Bear

NAT LOGAN

Table of Contents

Copyright & Registrations

This is a work of fiction. Names, places, characters and incidents are either the product of the author's imagination or are used fictitiously. Any resemblance to any actual persons, living or dead, events, organizations or locales is entirely coincidental.

Acknowledgements

Thank you to my PA for helping me see the light at the end of the tunnel when I was stuck trying to give Bear his happily ever after. Thank you to Leslee Sears Nevill, Gabi Brockelsby and Jayne Rushton for the dog names when I couldn't think of any names let alone the cute ones you all suggested. Thank you to all the readers who have fallen in love with the Bluff Creek Brotherhood MC and let me know how much you enjoy them. And last but certainly not least, thank you to my husband for letting me live my dream of writing. This book wouldn't have been possible without you. If you have any questions after reading the book, come find me in my reader group on FB Steamy Swoony Romance Reads and we can chat.

Now, grab a drink and settle back. The Bluff Creek Brotherhood MC and the world of the women of Franks and Daughters Bail Bonds are ready to take you on a ride.

Bear's Playlist

Drops of Jupiter (Tell Me), Train
Rescue, Lauren Daigle
Hold the Line, Toto
Someday, OneRepublic
This, Megan McKenna
I'll Be There for You, Meghan Trainor
Who Said, Hannah Montana
Little Bit Louder, Mimi Webb
Kiss Me, Dermot Kennedy
Umbrella, Rihanna, JAY-Z, Lindbergh Palace
One Shot, Hunter Hayes
One Good Woman, Peter Cetera
You Belong Here, Anberlin
Hold My Hand, Lady Gaga
Hope This Song is For You, Christopher
Honey, I'm So High, Christopher
Led Me To You, Christopher
A Beautiful Life, Christopher
Pick up the phone, Henry Moodie
Hard Days, Brantley Gilbert
Here I Go Again, Audra Mae
A Thousand Years, Christina Perri
Some Days, Brent Morgan
Here Comes The Sun, The Beatles
If You Close Your Eyes, Nate Bass
Fight Song, Rachel Platten
The Cape, Olivia Lane

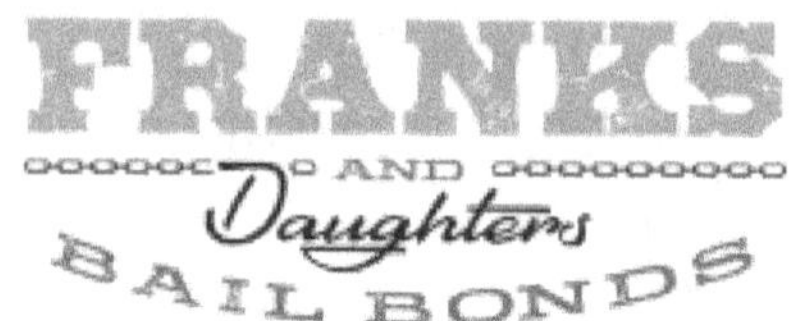

Codes

Code Monica: Everything's perfect. No injuries.

Code Ross: Everything's not okay. Help needed.

Code Janice: Going radio silent.

Code Rachel: Emotional backup needed. No questions asked.

Code Phoebe: Be ready with backup. Something's off but nothing pinpointed.

Code Chandler: Friendlies incoming.

Code Joey: Targets neutralized. Medical attention may be needed.

Code Burke: The old guys or originals have it.

Code Pancakes: The sisters lost their mom before the new codes were used. Pancakes were Kathryn's code for solving any problem. They'd meet around the table with pancakes and bacon and work through any problems. It stuck.

Code Marcel: Something's lost.

Code Balcony: Need some space.

Chapter One

Bear lay still, trying not to disturb the girl who was next to him. The faint light from the blinds let him see the top of her head nestled under his chin. He breathed in her scent. The unique one his brain told him was his safe, secure home. He flipped through his memories of last night, working to understand how they'd ended up like this. Not that he hadn't wanted her forever. Not wanted—craved. Being around her had become a compulsion because when she was near, peace and sunshine surrounded him. Not the platitude of let's all get along peace. No, it was that deep, sink into his soul peace where everything quieted and he could breathe. It seemed like he'd loved her forever.

The first time he recognized her as the woman she'd become, he'd been home on leave from the Army. He'd been thirty-three and she'd been twenty-three. The song he heard when he noticed her, "Drops of Jupiter," still made him think of that first glimpse of her whenever it played. She'd had on tight thigh- and butt-hugging jeans and a black tank top with the bail bonds logo on it in neon green, highlighting her small breasts. She had an athlete's body and even with her smaller breasts, he couldn't take his eyes off her, even though it was exactly where he had no business looking. He'd torn his eyes away when he'd realized she was Locks' middle daughter all grown up and the younger sister of his only female friend, Remington. She'd been grinning and laughing at something one of her sisters had said, flipping her hair over her shoulder. He wondered at the time what color to call it. Brown was too tame a term for the way the sunlight made it change colors. He'd craved walking over into her presence just to have a little of her sunshine. To bathe in the warmth of her presence for a little while.

The second time he'd denied himself, he'd been forty and she'd been thirty. He'd left the Army, joined the police force, and had made detective in the big city. Her family had been building a gym and wanted his expertise in planning for the unexpected. He was good at that—thinking of the worst-case scenario. It's how his brain worked. If he could think through all the worst things that could happen, he could plan for them. It helped him feel like he had a semblance of control over his life. One of the many little traumas his incubator had left him with. He'd helped on the gym plans all the while trying to not fall for her. Between her bringing him healthy food because she deemed he needed to eat better and her trying to get him to work out with her, he'd lost the battle. Lifting weights beside her, it was all he could do to keep his dick from having a life of its own. She wasn't like the women he usually picked up for a couple of nights. She was toned with small breasts, almost small enough to not need a bra, but it didn't stop him from wanting her. She was off limits—friend's little sister and daughter of an original in the MC. Plus, ten fucking years between them was a lot. He'd experienced things in the Army that had changed him and later as a police officer, he'd seen the worst of humanity. It might be ten years but he felt ancient next to her with her grin he craved to see.

He'd spent his whole life pushing down all the things most people dreamed about. Whenever he saw kids, he'd remind himself he couldn't chance passing along whatever screwed up genes caused his incubator to do the horrible things she'd done. He'd content himself with enjoying his friends' kids. He could be that favorite uncle who brought the kids all the cool toys and took them on fun adventures but was always on the outside. When he dreamed of a woman, he reminded himself it wasn't for him. He couldn't allow them to be in danger.

The third time he'd denied himself was when he and his friends had moved home for good to the MC, a little over three and a half months ago. Everything about her called to him but he was grumpy on his good days and downright snarly and unapproachable on his bad days—which happened a lot. She was a breath of fresh air on a hot, humid day. She'd walk into a room and he'd forget what he'd been irritated about. She was forever trying to get him to try one of her healthy creations. Most of them were edible and some of them actually tasted good, but it wasn't her food he hungered for. It was how she was the sun when he could only see darkness, but he couldn't take the chance he would ruin her. She deserved a world full of beauty.

Obviously, he was an asshole, though, because her head was lying on his shoulder, her silky hair tickling his neck, which is what had woken him. Her toned thigh was over his. His fingers itched to slide down and see if she was wet for him. Each time he'd reached for her during the night, she'd been ready and willing to do whatever he desired. The sounds she'd made when she came had him hardening, but he couldn't give in.

They'd been coming back from a three-day security gig. He'd kept it professional the whole time, though it had worn on him. He found himself gravitating close to her because she was one of the few women he enjoyed being around. She and her sisters hadn't given him an option but to let them in. He kept most at a distance.

They'd been driving back from Topeka when the tornado warning had come through. If they'd continued home, they'd drive right into the warning area. He wasn't willing to risk them both when it was dark, and they couldn't even see if something was coming. They'd found one room available with a queen-size bed. He'd decided he'd sleep on the floor because he wasn't sure he could keep his hands to himself. What an understatement. Holding her in his arms had started as a craving but built to a tsunami of need. It was all he could do to stop himself from reaching over in the SUV to feel her touch. Even a brush of her fingers soothed something in his soul.

When the thunderstorm had come through, he'd heard her whimper. She was so fucking strong, but thunderstorms and the threat of tornadoes freaked her out. He knew there was a reason he shouldn't crawl into bed with her but with her staring at him over the edge of the bed, her eyes pleading with him—his blood had all gone south, and he wasn't thinking clearly.

Winnie had asked him to come up on the bed. From there, he hadn't been able to resist. Her soft lips against his neck sent shivers down his spine. Her hand trailing down his torso, ruffling his chest hair as he held the most precious thing in the world against him. He'd held still—clenching his abs, resisting her siren's call. When her fingers had slid inside his briefs, tracing his piercings, he'd tried to hold back a moan but her touch had him turning and taking her lips. Lips clashing, her hardened nipples scraping against his chest. The first time had been fast. He'd kissed and tugged on her nipples, then made sure she was wet. She'd been soaked and when he notched his cock at her entrance, he'd paused, trying to hold back. Winnie's legs had wrapped around his hips, her hands grasping his shoulders, and when her voice had whispered, *please, Bear,* he'd quit fighting the urge to take her. Sliding inside the clasp of her pussy had him hoping he could hold back long enough to satisfy her. He wanted to savor his cock gliding in and out of the woman he'd dreamed of but it was too good.

Being inside Winnie had been heaven and he'd wanted to make it last but a couple thrusts of his hips had her clenching on him, groaning her release. He'd followed her over quickly, shouting out her name. He'd brushed a kiss across her forehead as he rolled to the side, snuggling her on his shoulder.

He could maybe forgive himself if it had been a one-off but after he'd had her once, he reached for her two more times. He'd had to taste her. Once he'd started, he couldn't taste her enough—her lips, her hardened nipples, and then her flat belly before he tugged her thighs apart. The smell of his woman had him diving in. She'd shivered when his beard brushed against her. At the first swipe of his tongue through her cleft he'd savored her flavor, knowing he'd never tasted anything better. Holding her thighs as they shook, he mentioned he loved her pretty pussy, and she'd detonated.

Each time Winnie had come, she'd whimpered his given name, Benton—not his road name. If he thought he wouldn't ruin her, he'd take her home and never let her go.

It had been the best night of his life, but he couldn't let it go on. She deserved sunshine, roses, and a family. His life wasn't for her. He'd known since he was a teenager that he wasn't taking a chance passing on his bad blood to anyone else. Rascal had been a wonderful father and if he was the only person in the picture, Bear might think differently, but he wasn't. Rascal had taken him away from his incubator. He didn't call her mother because she'd been the farthest thing from all that title entailed. She'd come back in his life multiple times and chaos always followed. If she thought someone was important to Bear, she wreaked devastation wherever she could. It was only a matter of time before she showed up at the Bluff Creek Brotherhood MC clubhouse and destroyed everything he'd built. With all his issues, he couldn't take the chance of ruining Winnie's life. She was better off without him but his chest hurt at the thought of inflicting pain. He rubbed the ache and inhaled her clean, feminine scent. He'd come to associate it with a home he always imagined.

She shifted against him, her nose burrowing into his neck. He dreamed of a life with Winnie but despite every scenario he imagined, they never got their happily ever after. Her dad, Locks, was an original member and definitely wouldn't want his daughter tainted by Bear's issues. He'd want a good man. Bear may have served in the Army and later served as a police officer and detective, but Locks knew where he'd come from. Bear couldn't see Locks wanting him or any of the baggage Bear brought with him tainting Winnie's life.

He'd get out of bed, go grab coffee and breakfast, then wake Winnie so they could get on the road. Maybe by the time he got back to the room, he'd be able to figure out what to say to her. How did he say we can't see or touch each other again, even though last night was the first time he felt whole? She was the elusive dream he yearned for but wasn't allowed to have. If he was a better man, he'd have held firm and never touched her, but he wasn't.

He gingerly moved until his pillow replaced his shoulder under Winnie's face. He craved to brush her hair back from her cheek and kiss her full lips but he couldn't. She was too perfect, too good, and she was worthy of a hero. He wasn't a hero. He'd come from a good man and an evil woman. His incubator reminded him every chance she had that he wasn't worth anything. Winnie was sunshine, light, and all that was good. He couldn't tarnish her life. She wasn't for him. She deserved so much better.

Chapter Two

Winnie finished dressing, thinking through everything that happened last night. She'd finally been with the man she'd crushed on since high school, fallen in love with in her twenties and finally had in her thirties. She didn't care what anyone said. He was the man she loved. He might have been ten years older, but he was the only man she could ever see herself with.

Sure, he was grumpy and sometimes snarly, but he was also over-the-top protective, examining every worst-case scenario. She saw that as a trait to admire. He was analytical, which kept their friends and family safe. She adored her gruff Bear. Last night, when Benton had finally given in to every dream she'd ever had, she'd hidden her tears.

Over the years, she'd taken every chance to show him the woman she'd become. Their conversations talking through safety measures for her gym had been the highlight of her days. She'd bugged Regina, the matriarch of the MC, to teach her how to make her cinnamon rolls because they were Bear's favorite. The added bonus of Bear spending a lot of time with Regina in the kitchen had been taken into consideration, too. Regina had been the positive mother figure Bear had needed when Rascal had taken custody of him. At least, that's what her sister, Remington, had told her. Being ten years younger than Bear meant she hadn't experienced Bear's younger years, but Winnie was an excellent listener, especially when people didn't know she was there.

Last night had been the first step in their journey to happiness. Feeling Benton inside her for the first time had been everything she'd ever imagined. The first steady push as he seated himself in her had her aching this morning for him again. She'd never had someone pierced inside her before. His piercing had rubbed her in all the right places until she called his name. His deep, dark voice while licking her folds and telling her he couldn't get enough of her pretty pussy had exceeded everything she'd imagined. When she'd come, she couldn't help but scream his name. She hadn't even realized she was going to call him Benton but when they'd been close, it had seemed right. She'd had sex before but with Benton, it was different and not just because of his freaking pubic piercing. It was because he was the man she'd dreamed of, though she was a fan of the piercing.

She wished the lights had been on last night because she'd imagined a hundred different ways to trace his tattoos with her tongue. She loved the tattoos on his arms and she knew he had the Bluff Creek Brotherhood MC logo because he'd gotten it as soon as he got out of the military. He'd added some over the years but most were hidden under his clothes. She'd wanted to see every part of him but she'd worried turning on the light might make him stop. She'd never been happy to hear a thunderstorm until last night. Her first whimper had been involuntary but she might have played it up a little when she heard him suck in his breath then call her name.

She couldn't see him feeling comfortable coming to her house with her dad's house being in the line of sight of hers. Maybe he'd be willing to come through the back way to her house or she'd even be willing to come to the clubhouse. She just wanted her man any way she could have him. She'd never been with a man with a beard and thinking about his beard brushing against her nipples then down her torso to her mound had her hoping Bear returned quickly. Maybe they'd have time for one more before they got on the road. Her stomach rumbled. She chuckled. Maybe she'd feed her other hunger first. She was starving.

She hoped Bear was out getting them breakfast. Although she was all about eating nutritionally and keeping in shape, she had a couple of vices. Coffee to get going in the morning was a must have and one of them but she didn't crave black coffee. Hers had to be flavored with either a French vanilla or caramel flavoring. She limited herself or she'd drink a whole pot by herself. The other was homemade caramels. It had been one of the treats her mom had made before she passed. After her death, Winnie and each of her sisters had picked up making their favorite things their mother made. It had taken her multiple tries, but Winnie had finally mastered homemade caramels. Her first tries were either too soft or hard as little bricks. As much as she and her sisters loved them, she limited how often she made them. They were such a treat Winnie could eat the whole pan in one sitting.

She glanced at the clock wondering how long Bear was going to take. She wanted to talk with him about what was next for them. They'd finally taken the step she'd been longing for. With her being the daughter of an original in the MC, Bear might not want to take their relationship public until he'd had a chance to speak with her dad. Locks loved his daughters and had always told them he wanted them to be happy. Bear made her ecstatic. Her dad's opinion meant a lot to her, but Winnie wasn't letting anyone keep her and Bear apart.

They still had an hour and a half to get home. The drive would provide plenty of time for her grumpy man to start sharing his feelings. She didn't expect his personality to change. She'd fallen in love with the grumpy man who analyzed all possibilities then had plans A through F to keep his family safe.

She couldn't wait for whatever was next. Marriage and kids were a ways down the road, but Bear would be a fantastic father. He was always helping out with Roam's kids. Multiple times, she'd found him in the MC clubhouse lying on the floor playing cars with Grant. She'd bide her time and let Bear move them at his own pace. Besides, as many times as he'd had her last night, her aching body needed a break. Her imagination had been sorely lacking because when Bear had stretched out between her legs, holding her thighs apart, she could have sworn it was an out-of-body experience. His full beard had been an added sensation against her thighs and core. She'd lost track of how many times his talented tongue and fingers had made her come. She'd worried she'd almost smothered him when she'd grabbed his hair and forced him closer. His lips had tilted up on the right, which was, for Bear, almost a smile.

The click of the lock had Winnie rushing toward the door. Bear pushed in, juggling coffees and a bag which had an amazing aroma wafting from it. Her man looked good this morning in his jeans and t-shirt tucked in. No MC cut today because none of the guys wore them on security jobs unless specifically requested by the client. She adored Bear in his cut but being able to see his t-shirt tight against his abs was a gift today.

"Here, let me help you," Winnie offered as she took the drinks, placing them on the small table in front of the room's window. "I was hoping you were bringing coffee. I need a little pick me up."

Bear opened the bag, placing a breakfast sandwich and napkin in front of where Winnie had sat along with a fruit cup. He fixed the coffee exactly how she liked and added something healthy to make her happy. He pulled out his sandwich and dropped into the chair. He was quiet, which wasn't unusual. Bear didn't fill the silence with empty words but this silence seemed different. Why was every nerve in Winnie's body screaming danger right now?

"See any storm damage while you were out?"

"Roads are clear. We can get out of here as soon as we're done eating," Bear grumbled.

Winnie wasn't sure what was going on. Bear seemed off from how he normally treated her. He was keeping his head down and refusing to look at her face. They'd been what she would call friends over the years, and they'd taken the next step last night. His demeanor screamed at her things were not what she had expected.

Winnie had always spoken her mind and she wasn't changing now. If he had an issue, they needed to talk through it.

"Is something wrong?"

Bear finally glanced at her, then down quickly. He'd taken a huge bite of sandwich and she was freaking positive it was so he wouldn't have to talk yet. As the middle sister of five, she had plenty of experience using silence to unnerve a person until they talked because they were uncomfortable. If Bear had a problem, he'd need to open his mouth because she wasn't leaving this motel room until he explained why he wasn't looking at her.

Bear finished chewing, finally looking her in the face. She recognized his look. Regret was in his eyes. Whether he had a pang of guilt because she was Locks' daughter, or he was remorseful about something else—she wasn't going to get the happy morning after experience.

"We can't do this."

"This?" She motioned back and forth between them.

"Having sex. Being a couple. We didn't think this through."

His eyes screamed for her to accept his words at face value but that wasn't who she was. She'd definitely thought it through. In fact that's all she'd done over the years.

"I did think this through. I've been attracted to you for the last twelve years. I fell in love with you eight years ago. Since you came home four and a half months ago, I've taken every opportunity to be around you. Last night wasn't just sex for me. It was finally having the man I love. I'm happy to slow this down if you need time. I'm always up for getting to know each other better through dates. I could fix dinner and we could watch a movie or just hang out."

Bear's eyes resembled a deer when the spotlight caught them—debating if it was flee or freeze time. She'd been around Bear enough to know she might have pushed him too far declaring her love. She was betting on fleeing. She could give him a little space, but it was definitely going to be a quiet ride back to Bluff Creek.

"I'm too old for you and I'm never having kids so we should consider this a lapse in judgment." Bear wadded up his trash, tossing it in the bin, and grabbed his duffle bag. He motioned with his head for Winnie to grab her stuff.

Hmm. The Bear had spoken and considered the matter closed. She could admit she was hurt. She'd been imagining him walking back in, grabbing her, throwing her on the bed and having his way with her one more time before they left because he couldn't get enough of her. His response hadn't been what she'd dreamed but it fit with Bear's personality. He'd analyzed their relationship and with his thinking couldn't imagine it succeeding. She'd take a little time to get over how much her heart hurt because she'd wanted him to wrap his arms around her and tell her she could have the fairy tale.

She'd grown up watching the princesses get rescued by the prince. Her sister Remington abhorred the word, but Winnie still liked it with a few changes. Maybe this one had a badass princess who kicked ass beside the prince and liberated him from a life of gray clouds. She could be both. Pretty like a princess but bossy like a queen. Her sisters called her a sunshine personality because she could almost always see the positive. Bear may think him shutting their relationship down was the end but someday, he'd look back and see today was the day the sunshine beckoned him into the light. And the interesting thing about sunlight is everything always looked better when it was bathed in it.

Chapter Three

Winnie watched the feeds, worried for Bear and her sister, Remington. When their security client had requested a change of location, Sarah, who was their sister and computer guru for their joint security company with the MC and Franks and Daughters Bail Bonds, had sent an SOS to have backup in Dodge City. Winnie and Beth, along with four of the MC members, had hauled ass and made the hour and a half drive in seventy minutes.

Beth had driven, which had left Winnie entirely too much time to think about the last week. Bear had ignored every text and call she'd sent. She'd even dropped in at the clubhouse trying to catch a glimpse of him. She'd need to check to see if he was watching surveillance. She'd supposedly missed him both times.

He might think ignoring her would work but he didn't know the woman she'd become. When she'd first been attracted to him, she chalked it up to a crush. She'd caught a glimpse of him when she was twenty-three. She'd brought a guy she'd met at a gym as her date to an MC party. It was the only time she went out with him. Once she saw the adult Bear, she'd known the guy she was with wasn't long-term dating material.

She'd admit she imagined Bear as the hero in any book she read and she read a lot. All her sisters did. When he'd consulted with her on the gym five years ago, she'd gotten to know him. They'd chatted online and he'd come to the property a couple of times. She had manufactured a couple of questions just to spend time with him.

Last week when her dreams had finally come true and he'd treated her like a woman, she'd known it wouldn't be an easy road. Although she was closest to Remington, Sarah had been the one she'd confided in this week. She was closer to Bear's age and could give Winnie some insight.

As she'd listened to Sarah talk about his birth mother, Winnie had known she and Bear's love story wasn't going to be easy. Was anything worth having easy? Winnie and her sisters had fought for every advance they made in their bail bonds business. Their dad, Locks, was their biggest cheerleader but he could only do so much.

The addition of the security company had brought its own share of problems. Clients sometimes ignored her and her sisters and only spoke to the male security personnel—not that she or her sisters allowed it to go on very long.

If Bear thought ignoring her for a week would make her give up, he was mistaken. People underestimated her sunshine personality. Her sunshine was a cloak around a will of steel. She'd set multiple goals over the years and met them all because she never quit. You only fail if you stop, and she never stopped.

"Anything?" War asked as he glanced at her screens. As president of the MC, he and Remington had been butting heads recently but he'd been fine to work with tonight.

Winnie shook her head. "No, but everything inside me is screaming something's off. Let's move next door to the bar in the hotel. I want to be closer."

War paid their tab and before the group walked into the hotel, he paused.

"Put on your vests. You can stage in the bar, but I want to be closer. I'm heading to the stairwell and staging on the floor below."

Winnie agreed. She slid her vest on, tightening it and checking her gun.

They split into two teams, going up both sets of stairs.

Code Ross - Three imminent.

Winnie's heart beat faster but she concentrated on doing her job. The code for help needed had them hurrying up the stairs. All the security people had watches which allowed texts to come through and had a panic alarm you could push to request emergency services. Winnie led her group into the hallway and spotted the lone gunman. She pulled and shot him but clipped his shoulder as someone else's bullet hit him, too. Beth and Cannon moved to confirm he was down as Winnie followed War into the room.

She catalogued the door had been blown with explosives, which indicated these weren't your average team. They had access to higher grade items.

The smell of gunfire hung in the air, but it was quiet. Too quiet. Winnie broke off to check the status of the downed man near the bar. She checked his pulse, not that she was expecting it. He'd taken a head shot. She shook her head, notifying War the man wouldn't be targeting them.

He motioned he was taking the lead into the bedroom. She checked the balcony door to see if it had been breached. It was still locked.

Bear: Code Joey. 2 targets neutralized. Holding bathroom.

She paused then ran toward the bathroom. Bear needed medical attention. War was in the doorway blocking her way in. She glanced around him and saw Remington pressing a towel against Bear's stomach.

"Flick, get in here."

Although they all had basic medical knowledge, as an EMT, Flick was best suited for the job. Remington moved once Flick had him and Winnie slid into Remington's place, waiting for Flick to tell her what to do. She looked in Bear's eyes. Despite being in pain, he was pleading with her not to say anything. He was in pain so she'd keep quiet. He was the priority right now, not her overwhelming need to kiss his lips to reassure herself he was still alive.

"Thanks for the backup. Flick, you'll go with Bear. Cannon, would you and Scoop stay with our client in the bedroom? War will be with me. Winnie, you're on police detail."

She wanted to scream at Remington but she couldn't blame her. Remington didn't know what Bear meant to her. It took everything she had in her to keep to their protocols and not argue with her sister.

She stepped back as the EMTs walked in and let Flick notify them what Bear's status was. She stood there, hurting that she couldn't hold his hand as they loaded him up. She swallowed because she wasn't going to let anyone see how upset she was. Later, when Bear was whole and strong, she could rip him a new one for not letting her share but for now, she had to compartmentalize her emotions. Put them in her little box for not right now. She'd pull them out when she was alone just like she'd learned to do on any job. Emotions caused mistakes and they couldn't afford any tonight.

It had taken longer than she wanted dealing with the police department. Despite the great working relationship their company had, the officers in charge had wanted to clarify everything before letting her go. When she'd received Remington's text after, Remington and War had interviewed the last survivor of the attackers, she'd been livid.

Client compromised. War taking witness to secondary. Keep client unaware.

It was all she could do to keep her face calm when he was giving his version of tonight's events. Listening to him throw the whole debacle on their security company and the MC, she'd wanted to toss him off the balcony. He was the reason Bear was hurt and if it was the last thing she did, the client would pay. She didn't care that he was a politician. He needed to pay for his part in this.

She'd been getting regular updates just like everyone was but she wanted more. Bear was in surgery and she was heading to the surgical waiting room. She'd been in such a rush that she'd taken the stairs. Pushing open the door, she hurried toward Rascal, Bear's dad.

"How is he?" Winnie barked. She sounded mad but she needed to know how her man was.

"In surgery. Come here, darlin,'" Rascal held an arm out and tugged her close as tears filled Winnie's eyes. His arms enveloped her and patted her back. "I'm sure he'll be his pessimistic, difficult self in no time at all."

Bear was pessimistic but his pessimism came out in the best ways on a security job. It was honestly one of the things she loved about him. He thought through everything and then they planned for them. Unfortunately, they'd never had a client request a secondary location and it was the one scenario they hadn't considered. She was positive within forty-eight hours of being awake, Bear would figure out a protocol to protect them from that.

"Family of Benton Carter?" a doctor questioned.

"I'm his dad," Rascal answered.

"He came through great. No vital organs were damaged, but he'll be kept overnight for sure. We'll be watching for infection, but I see no reason he shouldn't make a full recovery. He'll be in recovery then you'll be able to see him when he's in his room."

"Thank you, Doctor."

She sagged against Rascal, letting his arms hold her up. Growing up in the MC, Rascal had been a constant. He was the gruff biker who had a heart of gold and his son took after him. Rascal patted her back, leaning close to her ear.

"He's going to need you even when he pushes you away. My boy has always thought he didn't deserve the best but he does. Back when he was younger, I didn't think about having him talk to anyone about what he'd gone through. I wish I would have. I've watched you two tiptoe around each other the last few years. If he's your man, you'll have to fight for him, but I've got your back," Rascal whispered.

Knowing he understood what she was facing made it easier. She had someone besides Sarah on her side. Any of her other sisters would be on her side, too, but sometimes she wanted something just for herself.

Growing up, being the middle sister meant there was always someone around. She'd been so excited when her dad had talked about them having their own houses on the property. She loved the closeness of her sisters but she also adored not having to share everything or listen to every little thing that was wrong. Being in the different houses meant they didn't run next door with petty shit like they had when they'd all had bedrooms on the same floor.

Knowing Bear was going to be okay was a relief. She'd been petrified when he was shot and angry that she didn't have the right to ride in the ambulance with him.

Winnie recognized Bear loved her but he either didn't realize it or wasn't willing to face it. No man touched a woman the way he had—worshiping her body—without feeling something for the woman.

She'd made the decision to live up to her name, Winchester. Her dad had named her after one of the toughest and most dependable rifles. It was a little ironic that the Winchester rifle was one of the first repeating rifles. To win Bear's heart and convince him they had the right to a life together, Winnie realized she'd most likely have to repeat she wasn't running or leaving. He could run. He could hide, but just like when she was tracing a skip, she wouldn't give up until she had her man.

Chapter Four

Winnie parked the SUV and stared at the house. Rascal was going out of town for the night and would be back late Saturday. He was guest tattooing at a shop in Wichita. He'd asked her to either stay at his house with Bear or he would bring Bear to hers.

She'd opted for his because if they were at hers, Bear could leave. She'd dropped by a meal earlier in the week—Bear had grunted. She hadn't texted or called because she was giving him a little space. In the hospital, she'd been all gung-ho about winning him and one week in, she was getting irritated and a little depressed. Of course, it could be because she had the cramps. She was hurting, irritable and if he pissed her off, she might just do something she'd regret.

She'd run out of any sweets or chocolate at her house because she was a week early. She ate healthy but when she was on her period or was sick, she ate comfort food. This was one of those times when she wished she lived in a big city and not a small town. The only place left open that carried candy was the gas station and it didn't have what she liked.

Winnie grabbed her bags and locked the SUV, walking up to the door. Ringing the bell, she listened. She thought Rascal was waiting to leave until she arrived but the house seemed quiet.

The door was yanked open and Bear's scowling face stared at her. "What?"

"Where's Rascal?"

She'd much prefer to answer his question with Rascal around. Bear grumpy was one thing to deal with. The pissed off vibes that was almost suffocating her with its intensity was another.

"I'm here, Winnie," Rascal yelled as he strode toward the door. "I told you she's staying with you while I'm gone. We discussed this."

"No, you ordered. I'm fucking forty-five and don't need a babysitter," Bear growled.

Rascal rolled his eyes, shaking his head. "Oh, so it wasn't you that did too much and couldn't move yesterday morning? It wasn't you who moaned and begged for pain pills before you tried to get out of bed?"

"You know, other people have dads who support them—not ridicule them."

"Yeah, yeah, yeah. Grass is always greener shit. Sometimes parents have to tell their adult son to quit being a pussy and accept some help. Winnie, please come in. The second bedroom down the hall is ready for you."

"Um, sure."

Winnie wasn't sure what Rascal's plan was but ticking Bear off before he left didn't seem like the best idea. She hurried down the hall, aching with every step. Dropping her stuff off, she returned to what appeared to be a staring contest. She didn't feel well enough to wait forever on them.

"I'm hungry. Bear, have you eaten yet?"

Bear broke the stare, turning to Winnie and shaking his head.

"Okay, well, let me check out the kitchen and see our options."

"Regina dropped off chicken tortilla soup and some fresh bread," Bear commented, then reached his arms to gingerly hug Rascal. "I love you, old man, even when you meddle in my life."

Winnie turned and headed to the kitchen to heat up the soup.

Bear leaned back, comfortable against the couch. He and Winnie were sitting side by side with their feet resting on the large ottoman. If he wasn't enjoying the movie, he'd be closing his eyes because he was so comfortable. Regina's chicken tortilla soup had his stomach full.

He'd been irritated at Rascal's maneuvering but despite being achy, he'd enjoyed it. Being around Winnie made him happy.

Winnie didn't seem as comfortable. She'd eaten but she kept shifting around. A couple times she'd pressed on her stomach and winced. He wasn't sure what was going on but he was finding out. He paused the movie.

"Are you okay?"

She froze, turning to look at him. "Why do you ask?"

"Because you're shifting around and holding your stomach. Are you feeling sick?"

Her cheeks flushed and she looked everywhere but him. She almost seemed embarrassed, but why would she be?

"Um, my stomach is bothering me."

He turned toward her a little, wincing as his wound pulled. "Do you need something? I'm sure Rascal has every stomach remedy known to man. A lot of my worst-case scenario planning and always be prepared came from him."

"It's not that kind of stomachache."

If it wasn't that kind of stomachache, then what kind was it? Her hand rubbed her abdomen as she winced again. He stared in her eyes, trying to figure out what she was trying to say.

"Is there something that might make it feel better?" he questioned.

If anything, the question had her face getting redder, while the flush traveled down her neck.

"Do you have a heating pad? In my rush to pack, I forgot one."

He felt like the biggest fool not figuring out what was hurting but he didn't understand why she was embarrassed.

"Do you have cramps?"

Winnie glared at him, as if he shouldn't have brought it up. "Yes," she hissed.

"Sunshine, I've tasted every inch of you and had your thighs shaking against my face as you came. A period doesn't embarrass me and it shouldn't embarrass you. It's as natural as my boner every morning. Now, let me grab the heating pad. What else would help?"

"I don't want you getting it. I'm supposed to be helping you."

He ran his finger over Winnie's earnest face. This woman undid him.

"Sunshine, I'm getting up to go to the bathroom. I'll grab his heating pad and then you need to tell me if you need anything else."

He gingerly stood, using the couch arm to hoist himself up. His wound pulled like a bitch when he stood up or sat down, otherwise it was just uncomfortable. He went in the bathroom, took care of business, and headed to Rascal's room.

His dad had a bad back from bending over the tattoo chair for so many years. Rascal always had the heating pad he was using and a new one in a box.

He couldn't take away all the pain but he wanted Winnie to feel a little better. He'd text Regina and see if she had any thoughts.

Bear: Winnie is watching over me because Rascal thought I needed a babysitter. She has cramps. I'm getting her a heating pad but is there something else that could help?

Regina: I always liked hot tea and sweets—chocolate, cookies, etc. A couple of pain relievers might help too.

Bear: Thank you.

He walked into the kitchen, pulling open Rascal's sweets drawer. His dad didn't want them where he'd see them every day. Rascal had fought his weight his whole life but sometimes he wanted a sweet. Bear grabbed a bag of Sixlets because they were one of his favorites and a couple other bags to let her choose.

He walked in, handing her the heating pad then plugging it in for her. Sitting down on the couch, he opened the bag of Sixlets and held it out toward Winnie, silently asking if she wanted any.

She nodded, grinning, and grabbed a handful. "Thanks."

"You're welcome. I grabbed these, too, but if you want something else, I can have someone check the clubhouse kitchen. I don't want you hurting. Do you need any pain relievers?" He was irritated he had to deal with his pain but sheesh, women had to deal with cramps every month. He hated to see her hurting.

Winnie's hand reached over and patted his. "Thanks, Bear. I'm good now."

He settled back and flipped the movie back on. In his head, he knew he should never have kids because it wasn't safe, but he was a little disappointed Winnie wasn't pregnant with his baby. Which how fucked up was that? He didn't even know his own mind.

He needed to quit craving what he couldn't have and just enjoy what Winnie brought into his life. Maybe having Winnie here would help him sleep. The shooting had seemed to bring back his nightmares. He'd thought he'd gotten rid of them but they'd returned.

He'd been shot on the job years ago when he was training a rookie. Afterwards, he'd relived the shooting in his dreams for months, then it had gone away. For the last couple of nights, he'd woken from dreams of gunfire. What he could remember of them were a mishmash of dreams from his time in the military, the police force, and from when he lived with his incubator.

He'd never shared everything that had happened with anyone. It was easier to push it back and lock it in a corner to not think about it. Most of the time that worked but sometimes, it pushed through in his dreams. Last night, his incubator had done what she did best—terrorize him. She'd been the one holding the gun, threatening that she'd kill him if he bothered her again. In the dream, she'd shot the gun, hitting the floor near where he was sitting. In real life, she'd threatened him with the gun but then shot a watermelon she had on the table. After it exploded everywhere, she'd made him clean it up, reminding him that's what would happen to his head if he didn't keep quiet.

Chapter Five

Bear sat down with a cup of coffee, relishing sitting at the island and breathing in the smells of yeast, cinnamon, sugar and bread baking in the MC kitchen. The room had been updated over the years but it still had the huge island with chairs around it and a smaller table with six chairs in the corner. The coffee station had been enlarged over the years to include multiple machines, including a large one-hundred-cup pot. Coffee and the smells of baking were what he associated with his first real home. When he'd be away for so long, he'd make cinnamon rolls about twice a month to bring the smells into his apartment.

Regina had been called out to the farm for a question. He was in charge of making sure her cinnamon rolls didn't burn. She said she wanted to get his opinion on something when she was back. It was typical Regina—always a whirlwind. The restaurant-size refrigerator had a calendar on it where Regina not only had when and what was being served for the MC but now included who was watching Roam's kids and where they would be. He wasn't surprised everyone had stepped up to help Roam when his wife had left. It was what his MC did. They loved each other and held one another up when someone had fallen.

Even though Regina had aged, she was one of the most beautiful women he'd ever known. She was also the closest person he had to a mother. When he was growing up, it had been him, War, and War's twin, Roam. They'd been inseparable. Regina may have been their mom but she pulled him into her circle despite how wary he'd been as a kid.

After they'd left the Army, Roam had returned to the MC and joined Rascal at the tattoo shop. War and he had grown closer until he couldn't imagine not working with his best friend. War understood him sometimes better than he understood himself. They'd both missed Roam but had known Roam was never meant for law enforcement. Bear was glad his friend was getting to use his artistic gift because it was what fueled Roam. Bear loved the tattoos his friend had done for him.

He'd known as soon as War said he was done being a detective and was tired of their corrupt captain impeding their efforts to help victims, he'd leave, too. He'd honestly been ready before War but wasn't leaving War alone with no one to watch his back.

He glanced at his watch. He needed to check the cinnamon rolls. He pulled open the oven, pausing to let the heat escape then grabbing a potholder and sliding the rack out. He thumped the top of the middle cinnamon roll in the pan. It sprang back. Done, which was good. He was starving. At the rate he was going here, he'd need to up his workout after he was recovered. He was having a hell of a time resisting the sweets Regina kept on hand. Cinnamon rolls, dinner rolls and her croissants were out of this world. Pair them with the sandplums jelly and he'd gorge himself until he popped.

He slid them on the cooling rack, setting his time for frosting them. Cinnamon rolls had been the first treat Regina had taught him to make. She'd had all three boys helping around the island in the kitchen rolling out dough right after he'd first come. He must have been four or five. They'd helped roll the dough, then gotten to spread the filling, then roll the dough into a tube. He'd loved wrapping the string around the tube and pulling it to cut the rolls. When they'd come out of the oven and he'd gotten to frost and eat one, he'd realized Regina was different than his incubator. It had been the first time he'd realized he might be somewhere safe.

He still remembered being amazed there were snacks always available. In fact, Regina had them come into the kitchen in the morning and afternoon for healthy snacks but if they were hungry other times, they grabbed what they wanted.

Over the years, she'd helped deal with his tendency to always think the worst. She'd turned it from a flaw to an advantage. The first time was when she'd asked his opinion about her garden. She'd asked him to figure out a way for him to keep the rabbits from eating her vegetables without killing the rabbits. He chuckled remembering his multiple scenarios, but she listened to each of them. He loved her like a mom even though he'd never said the words.

Regina walking in and washing her hands pulled him from his thoughts.

"How's the wound healing?"

He obligingly lifted his shirt. Today, he was leaving it uncovered. Having the fabric rub against it wasn't bothering him.

She leaned over close. "Looks like it's healing well."

She turned, touched the top of a roll, grasped the frosting knife, and swiped the frosting across the rolls in five quick passes. He wondered how many thousands of cinnamon rolls she'd done the same to.

"Will you grab us a couple plates?"

Bear reached into the cabinet, placed two plates down for her to put the cinnamon rolls on, and got forks and napkins for them.

Regina motioned him to sit and then pushed his plate with two cinnamon rolls across the table.

"Thanks for waiting for me and watching the rolls."

He nodded, letting the sweetness of butter, brown sugar and cinnamon fill his mouth. This was one of the things he'd missed while he was away. The smell of bread baking, the taste of a cinnamon roll right from the oven, and the woman who had raised him smiling from across the table.

"These are just as good as I remember," he said, loving the smile that spread across her face at his compliment.

Her hand reached across, patting his. "Thank you. I can't tell you how happy it makes me to have all my boys home. I wanted to talk with you about the diner."

He heard something about the owner of the diner in town wanting to sell. Whatever Regina wanted, he'd do. He adored her.

"What can I help you with?"

"I'd like to look at reimagining it. It's been a diner for years. The town has grown some but the diner has stayed the same. I'd like to know the feasibility of adding on a small area which could sell some of our jams, jellies, desserts, and candies. I believe there's a market for it. I've roughly sketched what I'm thinking along with some of the needs I think this would create. I need your expertise thinking through all scenarios. Plus, you've grown up in the kitchen with me and know what might sell, too."

"Has the sale gone through yet?" Bear asked. They'd approved the purchase of it during council. It had actually been a formality. Regina and the MC had owned part of the diner back when he, War, and Roam were in elementary school. She'd sold her part with the right of first refusal back then because she chose to focus on the farm and their expanding family.

"We sign the papers today. If you feel good enough, I'd like you to go look at it today. There's also a building that has recently come empty between the diner and the tattoo shop. I can't get if off my mind that we need it, too, because what if the person who buys it isn't friendly to the MC?"

He stood up and cleaned up their plates, already running through the scenarios of what ifs. He leaned over, kissing Regina on the forehead. He might be a grump, but this woman had always been there for him. He needed to tell her out loud even though she most likely knew.

"I'll go check it out. Regina, I should have said something years ago but thanks for being the best mom I could have asked for. Love you," he whispered then turned and walked out the door.

She was the first woman he'd loved. Winnie's mom, Kathryn, had been a close second. They'd both worked to get the child who was scared of women touching him to open up. He honestly couldn't remember when he'd finally realized Regina and Kathryn only wanted what was best for him. He'd guessed it was probably when he looked forward to running in the kitchen and helping with the baking. His attitude had turned and the MC had become home.

Regina and Kathryn had even taught him to crochet in an effort to help him deal with his thoughts. He hadn't crocheted for years but now might be a good time to pick it back up. He'd look for the supplies and then settle back in a chair. Maybe he'd start a blanket for Regina for Christmas.

The MC was flush with money, especially with their portion of the security jobs. He'd rather they controlled the building between the two shops than worry about the what ifs. He was still on limited duty and was working to fill his time. Crocheting and thinking through what shops might prosper in that space seemed like the perfect use of his time. It would have the added bonus of keeping his mind off his sunbeam.

Chapter Six

Bear leaned back in the chair, waiting on War and the rest of the guys for council. A month since the shooting and they were still searching for why they were targeted. War had asked him to be here a little earlier and for once, he had no idea what his president wanted.

War pushed open the door, closing it and coming to sit beside Bear.

"How are you feeling, old man?"

He shook his head. They were the same fucking age, but War tried to insist because Bear was a couple months older that he was ancient.

"You're such a shit. I'm feeling better. It pulls a little but not enough to change my habits. How about you?"

War nodded and stared at Bear intently. "Good. I have a question to ask you before anyone gets here. First off, you are a phenomenal Sergeant at Arms. I love having you in that position but Rascal has indicated he wants to hand over his spot. I honestly think he stayed on as Vice President when Dad handed over the club just so it would be smooth. I've appreciated his insight but he wants to move out within the next six to nine months. Is that something you'd be interested in?"

Bear wasn't sure why his best friend was asking him that. He'd always assumed War's twin Roam would be Vice President.

"Am I missing something? Why not Roam?"

"It's his story to tell but at this time, Roam isn't in the place and doesn't want to be an officer. He's been offered it before and would prefer to stay a member without any officer responsibilities."

Bear started to think through all the pros and cons but then War held up his stand.

"We have been best friends forever. I know your personality almost as good as my own. There's no rush on this. Take your time and think it through along with all of the ramifications and we'll discuss again sometime in the next month."

Bear nodded. He could do that. He checked the time and pushed his chair back. He'd let the rest of the guys in so they could go over if they'd found out anything about why he'd been shot.

Having things to focus on helped him keep his mind off his sunbeam. He'd been thinking of different names for her, which was annoying in itself. Thinking about her only made him more confused. He craved being around her. When he was in her presence, peace flowed over him. They'd been around each other multiple times since she'd stayed the night to help him. They hadn't been alone, though.

They'd ended up having a Marvel movie marathon night and had fallen asleep beside each other on the couch. He'd woken up with her head leaning into his shoulder. Winnie was definitely a cuddler. He wished he had an easy answer. He was constantly torn because he knew eventually his incubator would be back to reign chaos into his life. Winnie was too sweet, too full of sunshine, to be exposed to his incubator's darkness.

Over the years, he'd considered sharing what she'd done to him with Rascal but whenever Bear brought her up, Rascal exploded. He'd been living in Bluff Creek six months and knew it was only a matter of time before she appeared. To make it a little harder, he'd moved most of his last bills to online and forwarded his mail to a post office box in Dodge City. They actually opened mail he received and sent him a picture through email. He'd done everything he could to slow her down but he'd come home. She'd figure it out eventually.

After everyone was seated and the doors closed, War called for reports. Everything was doing well but Bear had a hard time concentrating on them. He shuddered inwardly at the thought of Winnie having to deal with the woman who gave birth to him. Despite how much he wanted to bask in Winnie's presence and imagine a future with her, it wasn't for him. Trash wasn't allowed to dream of a future and his incubator had let him know he'd never be more than something to throw away.

Chapter Seven

Winnie smiled as she knocked on the door at Regina and Baron's house. When Regina had called and said the guys were gone and one of Roam's twins were fussy, Winnie had jumped at the chance to get out of her house.

Of course, she had to wait until War and Remi had left on their date. She'd helped her and her sisters deliver a warning to War. As she'd walked back to her house on the property, Sarah had walked with her and asked if she needed to talk. Winnie had told her no only because she'd known she and Regina would have a chance to talk. She did set up a time for her and Sarah to go book shopping. She was low on books and she needed more. Reading was helping to keep her mind off the man she wanted her own happily ever after with.

Regina Shields had been in her life as long as she could remember. Regina had been best friends with Winnie's mom before she passed. When her mom had died, Regina had kept Winnie's dad, Locks, and the sisters from drowning in the grief. Regina had also become more of a mother figure after they'd lost their mom. Winnie could ask her anything and Regina would help her work toward the answer. She hoped tonight might provide some clarity.

Regina opened the door, handing Winnie a crying Georgia before she had a chance to say anything. Regina strode back toward the hallway where Winnie could hear loud crying. Grant stood staring at her, wearing the large headphones he wore when he played his Mario game.

"Hey, buddy, tough night?" she questioned as she closed the door behind her, dropped her purse and held Georgia, patting her back.

He nodded, bugged his eyes out, then held up her pacifier. Once she'd taken it, he ran toward his bedroom. She could understand wanting to get away from his younger siblings. She'd been here less than two minutes and it was getting to her. The twins were adorable when they weren't crying—now, not so much.

She bounced Georgia as she held her on her hip, patting her back.

"Let's go see if Regina can help us figure out what's going on."

Winnie sat across from Regina sipping the drink she'd poured her. It had taken two hours but they'd finally gotten the twins calmed down and asleep. Regina had guessed it was teething because they'd been drooling and running slight fevers. After changing out wet, cold washcloths for them to chew on, they'd drifted off to sleep. Winnie had been surprised to find the twins' cribs set up side by side so they could reach each other if they wanted.

"Oh, I'd forgotten how hard it is with two of them when they're sick. Thank you for rescuing me. If I'd known they were feeling bad, the men would have never gotten to leave."

Winnie giggled at Regina's tone. She was positive they wouldn't have left either. Regina wasn't a shrinking violet. She was kind, loving, but there was no doubt, she wasn't one to cross.

"I'm glad I was available, but I certainly wouldn't have wanted to try to figure out what was wrong on my own. I love kids but don't have a lot of experience with sick ones. I'm sure Roam appreciates having you and Baron around."

Roam had moved back in with Regina and Baron when he'd come home earlier this year to a note from his wife saying she was gone and he could be a single father. Regina, Baron, and Roam juggled childcare along with the MC members, ensuring everyone could still work where they were needed.

"He appreciates us but he doesn't love us all living together. What man at forty-four wants to live with his parents? But it works for us. Now, tell me how you are."

Regina knew exactly how to get to the heart of everything. How was she? She wasn't sure but she knew what she wanted—Bear for the rest of her life.

"I'm confused," Winnie whispered.

Regina nodded, sipping her drink. Regina and Winnie's mom had both been experienced at waiting silently until one of them spilled all their secrets.

Winnie shook her head. "You and Mom could always get us to talk but this time, I want you to know I'm willingly asking for help. I don't know how to convince Bear we can be together. I'm always the one seeing the possibilities. Knowing that if we can get through the hard stuff, beauty is waiting for us. But that man has me ecstatic one moment because I believe I've broken through, then in the next instant, he's pulled the protective shell tight around him and I'm back to square one. If

I honestly thought he knew the way he was jerking me around, I'd knock some sense into him."

Winnie paused and swallowed around the lump in her throat. Her mom had been gone for a while and she'd gotten used to it—if that was possible. Days like today, though, when it involved a relationship and the man she wanted to marry, were agonizing. Regina was amazing but she'd give anything to have her mom sitting across the table, too.

"I don't know how to reach him. I know he wants me. His actions scream he loves me but it's like he's constantly telling himself he doesn't deserve me, if that makes sense."

Regina's hand reached across, grasping Winnie's.

"It makes perfect sense. I have loved on that boy almost as long as I have my own but he didn't make it easy. When Rascal brought him home for good, we hadn't moved into the house yet. Baron was expanding it so we could have enough room. Rascal lived in the clubhouse, too, with Bear. It was over a month before he was comfortable enough to be beside me while I was baking. I always talked as I entered a room, so he'd know a woman was coming in. He'd turn to face what could be a possible threat. I don't know what all that woman did but I know she didn't deserve the term mother. The first time he voluntarily slipped his little arm around my leg and hugged me, I sobbed after I left the room."

"I didn't realize. He seemed so strong going into the Army, then later when he became a police officer."

"Oh, honey, he is strong. Bear layered on piece by piece of armor so no one would ever hurt him again. He plans for every conceivable thing so he'll know how to respond. You know how they talk about how people are like onions and you have to peel the layers away?"

Winnie nodded. Her mom had used that analogy a lot when they were growing up.

"Well, Bear—he's not an onion. He's got layers but his layers are like my cinnamon rolls he likes so much. Each layer protects the softer, sweeter layer underneath. If you only had the cinnamon roll layers to break through, you'd be fine, but you don't. Bear has multiple hard protective layers on top of the sweet center—like a cinnamon roll encased in layers of steel, titanium, and rock."

"How do I get through that?"

"Honey, I know you grew up in the kitchen with your mama. Everybody knows that sometimes you need to apply a little heat. To break through, you're going to have to show him that it's okay to want you—to dream of being with you. Even the hardest metal falls when the right temperature is applied. Persistence, time and heat. Bear needs to know you won't give up on him when the going gets hard."

Maybe she'd just needed Regina's reminder that sometimes you had to fight for what you wanted. She'd never shied away from a fight before. Being part of Franks and Daughters Bail Bonds meant she'd gone against the odds before and beaten them.

Winnie needed to keep her eye on the goal—convincing Bear they could have it all. Hmm, a little heat might be just what they needed.

Chapter Eight

Winnie added another book to her basket then walked over to join Sarah. Sarah was standing in front of the bookshelves with a list.

"What's the list?"

Sarah turned and smiled. "It's Jesse's list. Beth said she was good because she would be doing surveillance this week and would grab books. Remington said she had a stack and would just borrow from me. Jesse, however, had some specific books she wanted."

Winnie glanced over the list then smiled at Sarah. "Hmm, little sis has gone down the dominant male rabbit hole it looks like."

"Yep. I've found two of them but not seeing this one she wants."

"If they don't have it, she could always order it and read the others first."

Sarah shook her head. "Nope, they're missing the first in series. These are later books."

"Maybe we can ask the clerk before we leave. I'm going to grab a coffee so we can sit and chat. Your usual?"

Sarah nodded and turned back to the shelves. Her sisters were all avid readers and since they rarely got to browse bookshelves, Winnie didn't mind Sarah's divided attention.

Getting their drinks, she sat down at the table and texted Sarah to join her. She'd grabbed them both a pastry. Book shopping deserved a little sweet. Winnie sipped her coffee and cut off a bite of the flaky pastry. White drizzles of frosting covered the turnover. She'd grabbed her favorite—an apple one—and had a cherry one waiting on Sarah.

Sarah sat down, dropping her basket with a clatter. Sipping her coffee, she hummed at the taste.

"Hey, we're in a bookstore. Let's keep the sex sounds to a minimum."

Sarah's eyes popped open. "Seriously? I'll have you know I sound way better than that when I have sex. At least, I think so. It's been such a dry spell I might be remembering wrong. I guess I'll just have to live vicariously through you."

Winnie grunted. "Yeah, if I was having any right now."

Sarah ate a bite of her pastry then swallowed. "Bear not falling in line?"

"No. Regina said I need to break through his layers but he's still avoiding me. How the heck do I show him I'm here no matter what?"

Sarah ate another bite, staring off over Winnie's shoulder. She loved her sisters but she was closer to Sarah and Remi. Sarah had that whole earth mother vibe going on. She was usually in sandals and skirts, sometimes heels if she wanted to feel pretty. She was their computer guru but also the woman that loved to cook and sew. Winnie was hoping her sister could help her come up with a plan for Bear.

"Okay, listening to what you've shared about what Bear said and watching him over the years, I think the biggest problem you have to overcome is Bear's lack of hope."

"Lack of hope?" She wasn't sure what Sarah meant.

"Bear has been let down his whole life. From the small amount I've gathered, his mom wasn't anything more than a vessel who gave birth to him. Rascal took him from her after neighbors called him when they heard crying from her house. She'd left him alone to go party. She'd left him with no food. I can't remember if he was three or four. They heard crying from the house. How hungry and scared would a four-year-old have to be to cry incessantly? It breaks my heart thinking about it.

"I think the only person Bear has to rely on is himself and probably the MC guys, or at least that's what the little kid inside him thinks. We all carry trauma from our childhood and adult life. Think how Mom's death affected each of us and we were adults. I think you have to be the aggressor and show him you're not leaving because he pushed you away. In the books we read, the guy showers the girl with gifts that mean something to them. Maybe you need to send or deliver some special things for him. He needs to know even though you're not with each other, he's on your mind. I can guarantee he's thinking about you."

Winnie thought through what she knew about Bear and what might make an impression on him while she and Sarah finished their coffee. Winnie wasn't running but she hadn't shown Bear she was still thinking about him. The more she considered how to heat things up and break through his armor, the more she liked Sarah's idea.

"Okay, I want to stop by the Harley Davidson store and one of the cake decorating stores for some cookie cutters. I might need your help frosting some cookies because you know mine look like a three-year-old frosted them."

Sarah laughed. "I could lie but we know it's true. Your gifts lie in other areas besides cookie frosting. I'm game. Let's pay for these books then go get your supplies to start knocking down Bear's walls."

Once her other sisters had heard they were making cookies, everyone had shown up. Sarah had suggested they use the main house's kitchen because it had two industrial-size ovens and twice the counter and island space for rolling out cookies and decorating. Winnie worked on piping the frosting around her lighthouse cookie. Sarah had illustrated three times how if she outlined it, then when she added the frosting inside it would be easier. Winnie was getting a little better. She hoped Bear appreciated the thought because her lighthouses still looked a little off.

Having her sisters all together filled that emotional well. The laughter, the teasing and hanging out were what she needed. Even though she wasn't discussing Bear with them, being closer reminded her she wasn't alone. Her sisters had her back. All she needed to do was ask.

She had such amazing memories of her and her sisters with their mom in this kitchen. Regina would join them sometimes, especially around Christmas to make candy.

Remington had three cookies done and they looked perfect. Of course she did. Winnie loved her sister but it would be great if her oldest sibling didn't do everything right. Jesse and Beth had decided no one could see their creations and had a two-inch binder opened and standing on its end. She wasn't sure what they were doing with their lighthouses but they were giggling and cackling while they worked.

"Hey, Remington, what kind of dick piercing does War have?"

Remington choked on the cookie she'd taken a bite of. Sarah pounded on her back, shaking her head at their younger sisters.

"What?" Remington choked out, reaching toward her glass of water.

"What kind of piercing does War have? We know he does and we know some of the other guys do, too."

Sarah scrutinized the younger sisters. "How do you know the other guys do, too, and which ones have them?"

Winnie was curious, too. She couldn't wait to hear their explanation. Jesse and Beth were definitely daring when they were together. Who knows what they'd done to get info on the MC guys.

She'd experienced Bear's firsthand, but they hadn't discussed his. Remi had mentioned War had lost a bet to Roam and informed them Roam had obviously cheated when they'd all lost to him, too. Of course, Winnie and her sisters had planned on getting belly button piercings all along. Remi even bought them all the cute pistol hanging from a chain so they'd all have something to commemorate working for the bail bonds company.

"One, because for some reason, everyone looks at me as a little sister and talks around me all the time. Two, we know War and Bear do. Scoop, Cannon, and Flick we don't know about since they didn't grow up here in the MC or serve with Roam, War, and Bear in the Army."

"Umm, he has a Jacob's ladder piercing if you have to know."

Jesse smiled and waggled her eyebrows at Beth. They giggled and bent down behind the binder. She wasn't sure what her siblings were doing because when Jesse and Beth got together things got a little wild.

"Done!" Beth and Jesse crowed and then held up their creations.

Winnie snorted, then laughed and chuckled until tears ran out her eyes. Only her sisters would turn their lighthouse cookies into dicks with correct jewelry for Remi's man. Jesse's even had hand lettering on it saying, "Lick me, Remi." Beth's had little lines which looked like veins. She'd added little black dots to his balls. Winnie wasn't sure if it was supposed to be hair or what exactly her sister had intended.

The harder she tried to stop laughing, the more she laughed. Even Sarah, who was probably appalled they'd ruined the lighthouses, was chuckling and wiping tears from her eyes. Remi was giggling and then motioned Jesse to give it to her. "I want to take a picture."

Jesse leaned over the binder to hand her the cookie as Locks walked in. "What's all the giggling about in here? It's good to hear my girls laughing and having fun."

Jesse and Beth's eyes bugged out. Jesse yanked her hand back and immediately started taking bites of her cookie, blocking it with her hand. Beth shoved hers in her mouth before Locks could see them. She chomped hers in two bites then choked on the two pieces, coughing as she tried to chew it. Jesse took smaller bites of her cookie but had her hands in front of her mouth, hiding her creation from Locks.

Locks walked around the counter and patted Beth's back. He grabbed a napkin and held it in front of her mouth. "Beth, just spit it out. You don't want to choke on it."

Winnie bit her lip and looked over at Sarah. Sarah was trying not to laugh and Winnie hoped she succeeded. If either Sarah or Remi laughed again, there was no way Winnie could keep her composure and she sure as shit was not explaining to her dad about dick cookies or their anatomically correct piercings. Beth shook her head, grabbing a glass of water and taking a drink.

"You all are adults. I know your mom drilled manners into you girls about sticking something too big in your mouth and choking."

Oh my! If her dad didn't shut up, Winnie was going to die of laughter. The fact he had no idea of the double meanings of his words made it even more hysterical. Beth finished the glass of water then wrapped her arm around Locks.

"I love you, Dad. You always look out for me."

Jesse had finished her cookie and was washing it down with milk. When Locks' head turned toward Winnie, Jesse mouthed *suck up* to Beth.

"Here, Dad, why don't you try one of mine? I'm not sure this one should see the light of day with my crappy decorating." Winnie held one of her less than perfect lighthouse cookies out to him. She wasn't sure if there were more dick cookies but she was not having her Dad see because the MC guys were the biggest gossips around. If one knew, then they all knew. Nuh-uh, no way.

Locks took the cookie and ate a bite off of it. He chewed, nodding his head. "That's really good. And since I took a normal sized bite I didn't choke, girls. I'm heading in to watch the weather. Try to not choke on any more cookies."

As the door closed behind Locks, they all broke into laughter again. It wasn't the first and it certainly wouldn't be the last time they hid something from their dad. She was hiding what she felt for Bear but she didn't need the MC guys making it any harder for her to convince Bear they were meant to be together. She'd have a darn near perfect life if she could convince her man he deserved a future with her.

Chapter Nine

Bear rode the roads back from Dodge City. War and some of the guys had visited their Texas Chapter while he'd stayed back. He was back to riding but he hadn't been up to a long ride, plus War had wanted him to complete a task.

His brother was head over heels in love with Remington. They'd gone from enemies to War couldn't stop talking about her and he could honestly see such a change in his friend. War was going to have everything Bear had ever dreamed of but was too chicken to work toward.

The drive had given him plenty of time to think about Winnie. She was stubborn. He'd found gifts and notes left on his bike this week. He carried each note in his billfold and read them multiple times a day. His favorite was the first, which she'd dropped off with lighthouse sugar cookies.

We all need light in our lives. Until you're ready to shine on your own, I'll be your beacon, calling you home.

The second and third were equally special to him and had been dropped off with the motorcycle fender lights he'd been contemplating at the shop.

Love doesn't make us weak—it binds the two together, strengthening them.

My love started as a glimmer but it's grown to a spotlight, showing me the way to happiness. Buckle up, Bear—the road might be rough to our happily ever after.

Winchester was determined and he wanted it all with her. He just wasn't sure he was ready to open her up to what his incubator might bring into their life. As he'd left the bar in

Dodge City, he'd been positive he'd seen her in a car. He'd followed but lost her at a red light. His glimpse was a reminder he wasn't ever going to live life without worrying about what his incubator might do.

Tonight was a fight night at the gym and he wanted to be back in time. He was taking the turn toward the gym road when a call came through. He didn't recognize the number but answered.

"Hello?"

"Code Ross at gym. Medical and fire notified. Repeat Code Ross. This message is a recording."

Code Ross was the bail bonds company code for everything's not okay. Help needed. Winnie and Remi would be at the gym getting everything ready. He'd been too preoccupied thinking about Winnie to notice the smoke hanging in the air. He pushed his motorcycle a little faster on the curve as sirens filled the air and straightened out as he took the road to the gym. He sped up on the straightaway and caught the ambulance pulling in to the scene.

He clocked War and Cannon using the thermal imaging camera they'd brought back from Texas. He didn't pray often but now, he was praying, pleading for Winnie to be okay. The gym was decimated with the fire. Although a couple walls were still partially standing, the back corner by the office was caved in. Bear ran across the parking lot to see if the camera was showing anything.

"Where's Winnie and Remi?"

War's face was devastated as he said, "We can't find anyone."

"Did you check the hatch?"

"What hatch?"

He'd never been happier he was a pessimistic grump than right now. He had to believe that Winnie had used the precautions he'd put in place and gotten out. He ran across the field, hopping the barbed wire fence. He pulled his gun as he spotted something on the ground.

Bear reached down and pulled a cap off the man's head. The man was holding his shoulder wound and was bleeding from the ankle. Not being part of the police force allowed Bear to do what he wanted, so he placed his boot on the ankle wound and stepped down.

"Ahhhh, stop!"

"Where are they?" Bear questioned, applying more pressure.

"I don't know and I'm not talking without a lawyer."

Bear chuckled darkly. His Winnie was missing and he'd do anything to find her okay. "Do you think I look like the person who is going to call a lawyer for you? Who shot you?"

"That bitch. I came out to make sure no one escaped. She came out of the lean-to and shot me."

"Cannon, tie him up and we'll talk with him later. War, come with me."

Bear ran into the lean-to and stepped around a four-foot cement wall blocking the back third of the structure. He leaned down, swept some straw away and punched in the code. Winnie had to be alive. If she'd been burned, the thermal imaging would have shown something. He waited for the beep indicating the hatch was unlocked.

"Come on."

Bear opened the hatch and shimmied down the metal ladder. He grabbed a flashlight and a two-way radio from the shelf. The hatch had dropped them down into the cement tunnels that ran from Franks and Daughters Bail Bonds property to the edge where the gym sat. Although motion sensor lights were supposed to come on as they passed different sensors, he wasn't taking any chances.

He flipped the two-way on.

"This is Bear. Code Chandler. I say again. Code Chandler. Holding at Crossroad."

"Code Joey. Evac site homestead."

Bear let out a breath. Code Joey was targets neutralized and medical needed. He grasped War's arm and shoved him into the waiting golf cart. The cement tunnels were ten feet wide which allowed the golf carts to turn around. He pressed the pedal to the floor. The golf cart jerked and took off. He was never so grateful for Jesse souping the carts up. He'd thought about running but with the added speed, taking the cart was faster. Plus War was a mess.

Not that Bear was any better but he had to believe Winnie would be okay until he saw her. He couldn't let his mind drift to all the horrible things that could have befallen her or he'd break down crying. His throat hurt trying to keep the tears in. He had to concentrate on getting there. The next crossroad should be the homestead. He just had to keep it together a little bit longer.

He stopped the golf cart and used the two-way to notify the homestead of their arrival. "Code Chandler. Entering homestead."

He didn't wait for a reply but punched in the code and shoved the hatch open as soon as it beeped. He clocked Remi and Winnie sitting on the medical beds but he only had eyes for Winnie. She had soot or dirt smeared on her face and a haphazard bandage on her arm, as if she'd done it herself.

Bear ran over and tried to pull Winnie closer for a hug. She batted his hand away. Her face tilted up to him and she shook her head.

"Bear, I'm barely holding it together. If you hug me, I'll lose it. I can't. I have to stay strong until we're alone."

He nodded at his badass little sunshine and realized the fire had cemented what he felt for her. He wanted her in his life. The worry about what his incubator would do hadn't gone away but he needed Winnie. He craved taking care of her and making sure she was okay. He wanted to protect her.

"Ambulance is here. Everyone is going to get checked out, no exceptions, but I want security," Locks directed. Now that Bear knew Winnie would be fine, he could check out the rest of the room. Locks had been standing in the doorway to the medical room in a bulletproof vest, holding a handgun with a rifle slung over his shoulder. Sarah and Beth were working the computers and monitoring the screens showing the homestead and surrounding area. "Jesse, what have you got?"

"I finished the upgrade on the first SUV. I could drive separately with War and Bear while Remi and Winnie go in the ambulance. You, Sarah, and Beth along with some of the MC could stay here. This was a coordinated attack. If I'd planned it, the burning of the gym would be wave one to get everyone distracted before I hit with wave two. Everyone needs to be on alert." Jesse's no-nonsense directions were exactly what Bear would have planned. He had no problem following her directions.

Flick and his partner came in. His eyes glanced around the room, cataloguing injuries. Bear knew the women would be okay when Flick's shoulders relaxed at the injuries.

Winchester stood up and Bear immediately grabbed her arm as she swayed. She was tough but he wasn't having her fall just to show how tough she was.

"I'm not going to fall but I wanted to thank you. Your analyzation of defenses for the gym which had us adding the hatch in the office is what saved us. If only we'd used you to help with our security protocols on adding new security people."

"Explain," Bear growled.

"Don't use that tone with me when my head is hurting. A new guy who was wearing one of our security shirts hit me over the head and knocked me out. I may be all sunshine and roses but I have no problem kicking you into next week when you piss me off."

Bear tried to control his anger but he wanted to go back out to the guy in the field and kick his ass now that he knew Winnie was okay. Hopefully, War would choose to offer him accommodations at the clubhouse until they could get more information from him.

"Winnie, we haven't hired any new people in security in the last thirty days. You've met all of them," Remington rasped out.

"This guy said Dad sent him and asked to help. When I turned to show him the boxes to move, something hit the back of my neck and head, and it was lights out. Luckily, the hot embers hitting my arm woke me up, otherwise the hatch wouldn't have mattered."

Winnie's words fed the fuel of his anger. They'd get the women checked out and then he was going to have a chat with the one they'd caught, then he'd start sifting through how someone got past security and with a shirt that should only be available to employees of the bail bonds and security company.

He followed Flick and his partner taking Winnie and Remi out. After they were back from the hospital, they'd be Code Pancakes. If he wasn't so upset about what had happened to Winnie, he'd be having a chuckle over War's response. If his friend had bothered to learn all the girls' codes, then he'd have a much easier life.

Winnie sat on the edge of the tub as Bear gathered supplies. He'd wrapped her arm in plastic wrap, not that she planned on getting her arm in the water. The rest of her might be covered in soot and smell like fire but the hospital had cleaned and disinfected her arm before applying the burn cream.

She was lucky—a little smoke inhalation, a small burn and a headache from hell. She had a small goose egg on the back of her head but no signs of concussion. Things could have been so much worse if she hadn't woken and gotten them through the hatch. When Bear had made the suggestion to connect the gym to their underground tunnels, she'd considered it a little overkill, but her dad had ordered the expense.

Things had been calm for so long with the business and the MC, she'd become complacent. Thank goodness, Bear and her dad hadn't.

"Sunbeam, can you raise your arms?" Bear asked as he grasped the bottom of her t-shirt, tugging it gently up. She raised her arms, stretching her neck. The back of her head hurt along with her neck. She'd love to have a shower and let the spray pound her neck but she wasn't allowed to get the bandage wet.

Bear got down on one knee, unbuttoning her jeans and tugging them off. He didn't wait for her to raise her hips. He lifted her with one hand, pulling them off with the other. His eyes ran over her. Knowing her Bear, he was cataloguing every injury, thinking through what he needed to do. He was her Benton when they were in bed making love but she could see the MC man Bear when he was in protective overdrive. His eyes met hers, his face coming closer. He brushed a kiss against her forehead.

"Let's get you in the tub." He helped her up, divested her of her bra and underwear, and was lifting her into the tub before she could help him. The warm water soothed her as she relaxed against the tub. The tub seemed pretty intimate and he was her Benton when they were just themselves. Benton's hand slid behind her, tucking a rolled towel at her neck.

"You relax, sunshine. I'll get you clean then we'll get you in bed with some meds."

She didn't remember the last time someone had taken care of her. She drifted, allowing Benton to wash her. She hoped there wasn't a second wave. She wasn't sure how much help she'd be. She didn't think the hospital would ever finish with their exams. By the time they'd gotten back and met for pancakes, she'd been holding it together by a thread.

Benton lifted her out of the bath and wrapped her in a towel. He held her steady while he pulled off his wet t-shirt and tossed it on the floor. She felt too crappy to appreciate her man's muscles on his chest or the tattoo over his heart with the MC insignia.

Sweeping her up into his arms, he carried her to the bed, laying her gently on the side. He slipped on her panties, sleep shorts and shirt, then handed her a couple of vanilla wafers.

"Eat those while I change, then you can take a pain pill before bed."

She chewed and took a couple sips of water as he changed clothes and then checked the door. He placed his gun on the bedside table, then handed her a pill. She swallowed it, watching his arms flex as he pulled back the covers. He clicked off the light as he settled in.

"Come here," he whispered.

Winnie let Benton cuddle her into his side, her head on his shoulder, his arms wrapped around her. She was safe and Benton would make sure she stayed that way. Normally, she'd want her gun beside her bed, too, but honestly, pills fucked her up. Her other sisters didn't seem to have the problem she did. Give her a pain pill and it was lights out.

"I was so fucking scared."

Winnie waited. With her head on his chest, she could feel Benton's heart pounding. He wasn't the only one who was scared. Coming to and seeing Remington knocked out beside her and flames all around them had petrified her. She'd known it was up to her to get them down into the tunnel. It had seemed like forever trying to get Remi awake enough to crawl over to the hatch.

"I've been such an ass pushing you away. I thought I was keeping you safe."

"Safe? What do you mean?" She really wanted to hear why he'd been pushing her away but she was so tired. She'd pushed through the adrenaline crash and continued to function because that's what she'd been trained to do. Her dad did extensive training before they were ever allowed to be lead on a job—bail bonds or security.

She'd wait as long as her man needed for him to open up. Even though her mom and Regina stepped in to help with Benton when he came to the MC, Rascal had been his dad. Rascal wasn't one to talk about his feelings or talk much at all. Sharing with her was something new for Benton. He'd get used to it because she didn't let things fester. She met them head on.

Between everything that had happened, the hot bath, the pain pill and being in his arms, she was having a hard time staying awake.

"Safe from the things that come with being around..."

His deep voice in the dark of the room was the last thing Winnie heard as she drifted off.

Chapter Ten

It had been a week since Winnie and Remi had escaped being burned alive. Bear had been called out the next morning for the MC and had to leave Winnie with a note. Holding her in his arms all night, her scent wrapping around him, had made him determined to do whatever it took to have her in his life. He wasn't sure how he was going to accomplish it but he'd do whatever it took to make her his.

He'd loved having her feel comfortable enough to fall asleep on his shoulder but he'd wanted to share what had held him back. He'd realized it was time to show Winnie what she meant to him. He'd been so busy trying to help keep everyone safe all by himself for so long, he'd ignored the huge MC family he had at his back.

If he and Winnie were going to have a life together, which they were, then it was time to open up and get help. He'd had flowers delivered which had cost him a whack. The closest flower shop was sixty miles away but it had been worth it.

Yesterday, he'd had an ice cream maker along with all the ingredients to make healthy ice cream delivered. He'd been chatting with Regina and she'd mentioned Winnie was looking at getting one because she was frustrated there weren't any healthy options around.

He'd also included a note inviting Winnie to dinner today in the empty building by the diner. He wanted to spend time with Winnie but also show her his plans. He'd never felt this way before—where he wanted to share his day and his plans with someone.

He'd been looking at the building yesterday and thinking about possibilities. He had to stop himself from calling her so many times to ask her opinion.

He'd never planned on falling in love with someone ten years younger but like her note had said, when she walked in, she pushed that glimmer of light into his life.

The glimmer built until his whole life was lit with her sunshine. She pushed back the doubts but with his personality, he still worried. She was it for him but could he keep her safe? Probably not alone, but it was time he used everything at his disposal.

"Bear? Are you here?"

Winnie's voice from downstairs had him walking toward the top of the stairs.

"Up here, Sunbeam."

Winnie's smile as she rushed up the stairs had him pulling her close. She had on her signature jeans that cupped every curve he loved, a v-neck t-shirt, which highlighted her delicate neck, and a leather jacket.

He slid his hand into her hair, tilting her head to reach her lips. He swept in, tasting his woman. The one who was meant for him. His Winnie wasn't an inactive participant. She stepped flush with him, rubbing her mound against him.

Seconds in her presence and he could pound nails with his dick. He needed to slow this down. He had a special evening planned and it would end with him inside her, but he was letting her know how special she was first.

"Woman, you go to my head and make me want to throw my plans out the window, but I'm denying myself until later."

Her giggle as she followed him brought a smirk to his face. He didn't smile. It wasn't a part of his personality, but being around his sunbeam had him wanting to be what she needed.

He wanted a picnic experience but the floors up here were rough and he wasn't going to chance splinters. He'd set up a round table with two chairs close together. Regina had given him a red-and-white-checked tablecloth. He'd strung strings of Edison lights from the rafters to create the mood. He had a playlist on his phone coming through a small speaker.

"Benton, it's beautiful."

He pulled out her chair, waiting until she sat to help her move closer. He walked to the warming area he'd set up and picked up the dishes.

"I tried to think of something I could make that you didn't get to have very often. I decided to see if one of your sisters could keep a secret."

Winnie smiled and his chest hurt with the feeling it gave him.

"It must not have been Jesse then because she can't keep secrets. I never tell her anything about birthdays or Christmas."

"No, not Jesse. Sarah suggested this. I made homemade Chinese food with fried rice, sweet 'n' sour chicken. Then I worried what if you didn't like how I made it, so I made her second item on the list which was salmon, avocado and cucumber sushi rolls."

"Oh, Benton, everything looks so good. Why is there one dish still covered?"

"Then I thought, what if she hates both, so I made the third thing on the list which was tacos with homemade salsa and guacamole."

Winnie leaned up toward Benton, tugging on the collar of his shirt, pulling him close. Her lips kissed his cheek as she whispered, "You are perfect."

He sat down and waited for Winnie to pick what she wanted on her plate before he did his. He waited until she took her first bite of food and realized this was a different feeling for him. He was content with just spending time with his woman. He could do this.

Bear waited until Winnie finished her last bite. He cleaned up their dishes then grasped her hand, leading her to the area he'd cleared. He waited until the next song started to pull her flush against him and sway to the music.

Winnie let Bear sway with her to the music then really listened to the music. She jerked her head and saw his smirk.

"You watched the show I wanted you to?"

"Of course. You couldn't stop talking about it."

She waited for Bear to continue then knew she'd need to prod him a little. "And?"

"It was good. I didn't like when he left her, though. That was a dick move."

She snuggled her head on his shoulder. Trust her man to be annoyed with a third act breakup. Winnie and all her sisters adored romance novels. They read more ebooks now because of the cost and convenience but Winnie wanted a library someday with the ladder she could roll along the bookshelves.

"Tonight has been perfect. I love your plans for the diner and the addition. Is this space going to be used? The lights with the rafters are very romantic."

Bear brushed a kiss against her forehead then twirled her away from him then back snug against him. Being in his arms could become addicting but she was okay with that. She'd loved him for years and he was finally coming to terms with their love. Bear wouldn't admit it yet because he'd been conditioned to doubt everything.

He'd need time, which was why she wanted to keep this just between them. Besides Regina and Sarah, no one knew and she was planning on keeping it that way. Bear could think it was because she wanted to keep everything to herself but she was doing it for him.

She was giving him what he needed—time. Time to come to terms with their love and that he could trust her. The MC was a huge family that she loved deeply but there were downsides. If the guys knew they were dating, there'd be teasing. Her dad and Rascal would push Bear to make a statement—to claim her. She wanted to be claimed but she wanted it to be because Bear couldn't live without her, not forced into it because she was the daughter of one of the original members.

She breathed in Bear's scent. He smelled of the outdoors and a bakery. The yeasty smell that made your stomach rumble and want to dive into a pastry.

"Are you sniffing me?"

She giggled. "Maybe. I like smelling you."

His lips caressed her cheek and trailed kisses down her neck. "You keep smelling me. I'm feeling a little peckish. I think I need to try out my dessert."

His hands coasted down, sliding underneath her shirt. His touch against her stomach had her breathing deep. He paused, glanced around, then slid an arm under her leg, lifting her.

"The floor's rough but that table looks perfect to lay you down on and feast."

He sat her on the table, turned and grabbed the tablecloth, and laid it down. Lifting her, he situated her then reached for her neck, pulling her closer. Knowing her guy, he'd thought through ten scenarios of bad things that could happen if he just pulled her clothes off on the dusty table. She didn't care. She loved everything about him, except maybe she could get him moving a little faster. He hadn't been inside her since that first time and almost three months was too long to go without her man. Thank goodness he finally pulled his head out of his ass.

Winnie cupped Benton's hardness, sliding her finger up and down the length through his jeans. "I want you, Benton." His hands helped her lie back, then efficiently had her boots, jeans and panties off and folded on the floor.

Then he paused and pulled her back up. His hand slid into her hair as his lips claimed hers. The kiss went on as she tried to get closer to Bear. She wanted him against her. When his lips pulled away, he'd already divested her of her shirt and bra.

"I couldn't not see those gorgeous breasts as I feasted."

Winnie looked down at her chest, brushing a finger along her side. She'd come to terms with her less than big chest. Bear seemed to enjoy her in the hotel but she still felt inadequate compared to others.

"They're not very big."

Bear shook his head. "Winnie, you're fucking perfect. You are beautiful. You're a badass bounty hunter who helps others defend themselves."

He grasped her thighs, pulling her to the edge and holding them apart. His eyes trailed from her breasts down to her mound.

"Now, let me taste some of my sunbeam. Feel free to make as much noise as you want because no one's in the building, plus I've got an in with the manager."

His warm breath heralded his tongue tracing close to her center. A shiver raced through her. She dropped her head back and let herself enjoy. It had been too long and feeling his tongue tracing her had her shaking. His beard brushing against her was an added sensation she'd missed. His finger traced around her core then slid in. She'd waited so long to have her Benton but he was hers now. His beard, his tongue and his finger touching her had her exploding. Her legs shook as fireworks exploded behind her eyelids.

Once she came down, she grasped his hair. "Now, inside me."

"Sunbeam, you have a couple more in you."

She tugged harder on his hair. "Maybe, but I've missed you. I want your cock."

His lips tilted in a smirk. "Okay, my sunbeam gets want she wants."

He was unzipped with his underwear and jeans pushed down past his ass in no time. His cock was hard, weeping and dark red. In fact, it looked a tad painful. She could definitely help with that. Winnie leaned up a little until she could wrap her hand around it, sliding her finger over the pulsing veins.

"Just so you know, I'm not going to promise to last. You're the only one I've ever been bare inside and woman, you make me lose control."

Winnie scooted her butt closer to the edge, widening her thighs to accommodate Benton's hips. "That's okay. You have a good recovery time."

Benton lifted her leg and held it as she notched him at her entrance. His other hand slid into her hair, tilting her head down to watch him enter her. He pushed in a little then pulled out again. He was good sized and she was wet but he still needed to work himself in.

His cock glistened with her moisture as he pulled out. It was so hot to watch his cock gliding in and out of her. He loved how her pussy felt clamping on his. His next thrust in had her moaning.

"There's that sound I wanted. You're so sexy when you can't be quiet."

Benton pulled out, snapping his hips and filling her again. She wasn't the only one making sounds. Benton grunted as he slid the last way in.

"I can't make this last. Your pussy's sucking me in and feels too good."

Winnie clenched around him, feeling every inch of him curling her toes.

"That's not helping."

"I'm so fucking close, Bear. Faster, please."

Winnie leaned back as Benton powered inside her. Each thrust in rubbed the spot she'd never been able to find on her own no matter how many times she tried.

"Oh fuck, Sunbeam. Please fucking come." Benton's groan accompanied his thumb rubbing her clit. She closed her eyes and shook as she went over. Her man followed with one last thrust and called her name as he came inside her.

She was exactly where she was supposed to be, with her man inside of her and his hand holding her cheek. She'd worry about the clean up without a condom later because having him without a layer between them was worth anything.

Chapter Eleven

Winnie pulled the plastic wrap off her tray and put it on the lunch table. Regina and Remington had lunch running ahead and there wasn't anything for Winnie to do. She couldn't quite decide if she should try to sit by Bear or if it would be too hard to hide how she felt for him.

Some may think it was stupid to keep their relationship a secret but she had two pretty big reasons. First, Bear had just done an about face and decided he wanted a relationship. She knew what the MC guys were like. She'd watched them tease and torment the guys in a new relationship. She planned on having a life with Bear and wasn't having any of them scare him off with all their bantering. Second, being the middle daughter, she'd always had to share or compete with her sisters. She wanted Bear to herself for just a little while. No one expecting certain things from their relationship and no one giving their opinion. They were both adults and didn't need anyone meddling. Sarah knew but she wasn't one to tease at all. She was the most mature and nurturing of all of them.

Bear came in with some of the guys. He said hi to her and her sisters then let the other guys find seats first. Of the five left, he took one of the ones beside her. When he scooted his chair in, he brushed his hand across the top of hers. A featherlight touch that had her squirming in her seat.

Baron waited until everyone was seated then said the blessing. Regina had made her gravy steak—at least that's what Locks called it. Winnie loved it because it cooked in the gravy for over two hours and was so tender, she didn't need a knife to cut it. Plus the gravy over mashed potatoes was so good. She'd need to run extra with all the carbs, but she didn't indulge often.

Bear handed her the bowl of potatoes and let her grab a scoop before he got his. Then he held the platter with the steaks and gravy while she took a portion then got his before giving it to her to pass on. The dinner rolls came by along with corn, green beans, fried okra and a salad. Each time, he held the items he knew she liked.

At first, she'd thought he was holding everything but then realized it was only her favorites.

"Dude, you've had three. Why don't you share with the rest of us?" Cannon griped.

"Well, I was just trying to help you out. You look like you're getting a little thick around the middle. Maybe you should spend more time running the range than working behind the counter." Scoop grinned, delivering the comeback.

Bear reached between them, grabbing the tray. He turned and handed the last piece of vegetable pizza she'd brought to her. She did love her veggie pizza and Bear had no idea she'd kept a half pan at her house.

"Oh, for Pete's sake, she brought them. She can make them anytime," Cannon whined.

Bear had been sweet enough to get the last piece for her and she wasn't going to let his good deed go to waste. She picked up the piece like she was going to give it to them, then pulled it apart into two. She popped one piece in her mouth and gave the other piece to Bear.

"Man, you are just mean, Winchester. See if I let you know when anything special comes into the range." Cannon scowled when he threatened her.

"Man, are we an MC having lunch or a bunch of whiny girls?" Roam remarked, helping feed Georgia. When no one said anything, he looked around the table as the silence continued.

Winnie waited to see if Regina was going to get after him. She couldn't imagine he'd fare any better than War had when they'd disparaged women.

"Oh, Daddy, Nana's face is getting red. It only gets red when she's mad. You should say you're sorry or you might have to go to time out."

Grant's whispered words, which everyone at the table could hear, had Winnie trying to stifle a giggle. Bear's hand underneath the tablecloth slid along her thigh and squeezed lightly. She went from needing to giggle to wanting to find a closet to have a little alone time with Bear.

"Grant, I didn't even realize how my words sounded. I'm so sorry."

Roam's exaggerated tone had Regina shaking her head at him and his brothers whispered *suck up* under their breaths. Winnie squeezed her legs together than flicked Bear's fingers. Someone was going to notice something and she didn't want that. Bear's secret touch letting her know he wanted her meant everything.

Chapter Twelve

B ear clocked Scoop's nod and headed out to what looked like a storage shed for their winter snowmobiles and other items. Most people ignored it and Bear had always wondered if Baron had shared about his special room below the shed.

Of course, after the attack on the gym, the average person would assume the hatch led to another tunnel the MC and bail bonds had built, which was semi-true. The hatch did lead to a tunnel but this tunnel and area didn't connect to any of the other escape tunnels. It led to a hatch on the back side of Regina's garden that was hidden underneath a small barn that housed the MC's snowplow.

Bear slid down the ladder, forgoing the steps. He was in a hurry. He was a little proud of himself waiting until now but Scoop and Cannon had convinced him a little time in a jail cell might make their prisoner more talkative.

War had no idea the guys were having a chat tonight with their prisoner. War was torn. He talked about getting the bad guys who the law would never touch but he still had that core who believed everyone deserved a chance. Bear had grown up with his incubator always coming in and destroying everything he'd built or taking his savings to leave him alone.

Right and wrong were all good and well when there weren't dirty cops or people able to pay their way out of any crime. Bear considered sometimes for the greater good a person might need to step into the gray area to accomplish his goals of protecting his family.

Scoop opened the metal door where their guest had been staying. He had a composting toilet, bottled water available, a thin mattress and blanket on the floor, and he was given three meals a day. Their guest hadn't seen the sun or a clock. They'd varied when they turned off the lights and fed him actually more than three meals a day to make him think a longer time had passed. Flick had patched him up and made sure he didn't need a hospital.

Scoop had done a deep dive on their guest using facial recognition because surprise, surprise, his fingerprints had been burned off.

Bear waited, staring at their guest while Scoop and Cannon secured him to a metal chair that had been nailed into the concrete. His guest didn't appear scared. Having food and a place to sleep had given him a sense that they weren't going to hurt him. Bear tilted his head, studying the man in the silence.

"You need to let me go."

This guy may have had his fingerprints removed but he'd only lasted a couple minutes before blurting something out. A professional would have lasted longer. Maybe this would be easier than he thought, which kind of pissed him off. He had a lot of anger bottled up from seeing his woman hurt and her gym burned to the ground. He'd like a chance to work it off.

"Why?" Bear worked to keep his tone bored, which was fucking hard since bored was the last thing he felt. All-consuming rage still coursed through him two and half weeks after he'd almost lost Winnie.

"The people I work for will kill you all."

Now that just really pissed him off. Was the guy not going to withhold information? How would he justify hitting him if he cooperated?

"Oh, your people? Your people that have no idea where you are and probably think you're dead? Yeah, I'm sure they didn't give you a second thought after you screwed up your mission. Yep, you failed."

Their guest's face reddened and a little vein pounded in his neck.

"Why would they care about someone who was on probation for check fraud? It's not like you're this big bad criminal who's an integral part of their operation." Scoop scoffed. "What, was the A team of your group not available, so they had to make do with you? What are you, C or D team?"

"I'm important and you don't know who you're messing with."

"Seriously, could we move this along? I'm getting bored. You guys made me dig that freaking hole and since you wanted it quiet, I had to do it by myself. Do you guys know how long it takes to dig a big enough hole for a body?" Cannon even whined a little at the end to make it believable.

He and the guys hadn't gone over what they were going to say but they'd all worked together enough they could depend on each other. Cannon was excellent at reading people's smallest expressions and knowing exactly when in an interrogation to pull out their greatest fear.

A couple beads of sweat were appearing on their guest's forehead but he didn't seem in a hurry to say anything.

"I'm not wasting my time if he's not going to help us. Go ahead and take him, Cannon. It's dark enough, just tie his hands and feet, stuff a cloth in his mouth and cover him with the dirt. He'll suffocate before it's light tomorrow morning."

Bear turned away while Cannon and Scoop unhooked him from the chair. He was really wanting to hit the guy so he provided an opportunity. Their guest hit Cannon in the stomach and elbowed Scoop in the neck. Both the guys pretended like they were down because the one thing they had talked about was Bear wanted to pound on their guest a little.

Bear turned before their guest could hit him from behind and landed a hard left, followed up by a right punch into his stomach. When their guest bent over holding his stomach, Bear decided he needed to teach a little more of a lesson. Grabbing him by his hair, Bear held his head upright and landed a direct punch to his face, knocking him out.

"Ahh, I thought you'd play with him a little longer. That was a little anticlimactic," Scoop commented.

"I was worried if I gave myself free rein I wouldn't be able to stop. Nice touch with the digging the hole."

Cannon chuckled. "Thanks, I'm thinking we splash water on him and wake him up. Then Scoop and I drag him to the other hatch. I think he'll give us all the information we need."

"Since I know we aren't burying him on the property, what did you and Scoop come up with to get him out of here before we go on lockdown with everyone?"

"He has a warrant out of Texas for a felony. Jesse and Beth are meeting us at the hatch and will drive into Oklahoma about an hour and meet a friend they have who will take our guest to Texas and turn him in. She's making Jesse hit her so she can say she was hurt when she tried to defend herself."

Leave it to his friends to not only have his back but arrange it in a way that whoever he was working for would think he'd been killed or just disappeared. Hopefully, the information Scoop and Cannon would find out could help them defend themselves.

Chapter Thirteen

W innie glanced at the plans and waited for Bear to arrive. She hated losing the gym because she'd put her blood, sweat and tears into making it a reality. She'd vowed that when they rebuilt, it would be better than before.

When Beth had come up with the idea of buying the land between the MC and the bail bonds, over 3640 acres, Winnie had breathed a sigh of relief. She loved the idea of the gym being better protected. She'd also been able to add parking spaces which couldn't be seen from the road. If someone around wanted to come take defense lessons and not have anyone see them, their car could be hidden and Winnie could do a private lesson.

She'd been amazed at how fast Gage's construction crew from the MC's Texas chapter had finished even with all the underground additions. Since that underground addition at the previous gym had saved her and Remington's lives, she was fine with multiple egresses from the gym.

Bear had suggested a panic room which was fireproof and was on the other side of the gym from the egress. He had multiple ways for them to leave the building. Her favorite had to be the crawl space he'd added between the outside wall and inside walls. Both of the locker rooms had secret doors installed to allow an escape.

Keeping her and Bear's relationship a secret the last two months since the fire had been hard but they both needed the time. Next week was Halloween and the MC was having a huge party. She'd volunteered to watch Roam's kids. Her reasoning had been so he could attend and Regina and Baron could also. She hadn't wanted to be at a party and not get to dance with Bear. The positives outweighed the negatives on keeping their relationship a secret but there were times she second guessed herself. Then she'd watch one of the brothers giving War crap and realize she'd put up with anything.

Thank goodness the pranks seemed to have calmed down. You could definitely tell which sisters enjoyed that. Jesse and Beth had jumped in and made some enemies of the guys. Winnie was fortunate none of the pranks had been directed at her. She wasn't challenging Bear in pranks. His brain would be way too devious thinking up paybacks. Nuh-uh, no way.

Winnie and Bear had one more walk through and then Sarah would test all the alarms, cameras, etc. Winnie was positive Sarah had already done that. Her sister was too organized not to.

"Hey, Winnie, we're here. Where are you?"

Winnie walked out the office wondering why Sarah's voice was calling for her.

Sarah and Bear were walking across the gym floor. Bear dropped back a little, shrugging his shoulders. Sarah's grin let her know her sister was messing with her.

"I dropped by to pick up some sweets and Bear said he was headed here to go over the building. I thought why not come and do my stuff now."

Sarah's voice might be all sickening sweet but Winnie knew better. Sarah was who Winnie had shared about Bear with and Sarah freaking knew Winnie was giving Bear time by keeping it quiet. As her older sister, though, she couldn't keep from nosing in and getting her point across.

Sarah had been urging her for weeks to come clean to the MC. The longer it went on the more chance someone would catch them. Sarah had even admitted it shouldn't be like that but despite Locks seeing them as capable, fierce woman in the company, he was old-fashioned on dating.

Winnie didn't care what her dad's views were. She was thirty-five years old and she wasn't getting permission from anyone to date a brother in the MC. She got all the stuff about how it was respect. They had a brotherhood and relied on each other but although she loved and respected her dad, she was not property of anyone but herself. She gave herself to Bear and when she accepted his property cut, it would be because they owned each other's hearts.

She led her nosy sister and the man who she loved with all her heart over to the plans and their check off list for ensuring the gym was up to code and ready for inspection.

Bear walked by her, brushing his index finger against hers as he passed. His small touch reminded her with Bear she'd found a man who would always be by her side. She'd never be on her own because Bear would always have her back. He was her protector but he didn't diminish her strength.

She'd almost lost hope over the years if he'd ever come home and ever notice the woman she was. Dragging out the planning of the gym initially had given her that spark of hope he saw her as a woman. She'd notice the interest in his eyes before he'd look somewhere else. She'd be forever grateful they'd had a security detail together. Sometimes fate needed a little help moving things along.

Chapter Fourteen

Tonight was going to be unbearable. Watching Winnie receive congratulations on the gym opening and unable to stand beside her with his arm around her.

His sunbeam had burrowed into every facet of his life until he couldn't imagine a day without her. She pushed his grumpy ass when he slipped into his dark days, which with Winnie around were fewer. Her hand on his chest and her whispering his name had brought him back so many times when he started to analyze everything.

He checked his phone to see if she'd texted back. He wanted to know if he could see her for just a few minutes before the opening. It was a momentous occasion for his woman. She'd rebuilt from the ashes—literally. He was thankful the purchase of the additional land had gone through. Having the gym between the MC main compound and the bail bonds compound made it infinitely safer.

He hoped they came up with a better way to refer to everything. It might as well all be the Bluff Creek Brotherhood compound because Locks didn't hide his affiliation with the MC anymore. Times had changed and the bias against motorcycle clubs, especially ones like theirs, wasn't quite as negative.

Technically, if he had his way, the entire acreage they owned would be combined into one big area with a barrier to keep anyone from entering it without them knowing. He'd looked over Beth's original plans and with a little tweaking he believed they'd have a safe place for all of them. He'd jotted down a couple additions he'd like to use to increase their security. There were a couple of weaknesses he'd spotted and they'd bother him like an itch under his skin until he resolved them.

The information Cannon had gotten from their guest before he left hadn't sparked any threads Scoop could follow. Their guest had mentioned a woman whom he spoke to but was never told her name or saw her. Scoop and Sarah were both excellent with ferreting out information but they needed something to start their search with and the leads were slim. His phone beeped.

Winnie: On my way

He hoped she liked her gift. Trying to figure out something to celebrate the gym's reopening while not letting anyone know they were dating was almost impossible. He made a list of pros and cons for the items he'd been considering. This one seemed to be one that Winnie would cherish but would also pass as the gift of someone close to the sisters as opposed to the gift of a lover.

Winnie's front door opened and her steps were quiet on the floor. His woman loved her different athletic shoes. He wondered how she planned on dressing for the opening. He liked her best in her leggings and athletic shoes, or her jeans that highlighted every smooth muscle in her thighs with motorcycle boots. She was perfect for him.

Winnie dropped her jacket and walked straight to him, pulling his head down for a kiss. Winnie's lips felt cool against his as she kissed him. Each time he felt her lips against his and held her in his arms, he thanked God he came back to Bluff Creek and Winnie.

Winnie leaned back, gazing in his eyes. "I needed that. I have about ten minutes to change clothes and see you then head back. Remi looked at me like I was crazy to not wear the correct clothes."

He chuckled. He was surprised with how astute her sisters were that they all hadn't realized something was going on. "I have a gift for you. I, ah…" He paused. Winnie didn't need all the reasons he did or didn't pick this gift.

"Oh, gimme, gimme." Winnie bounced up and down, holding her hands out. He handed her the present and watched her sit on the bed to tear into it.

When she had it open, she ran her fingers across the top of it. Winnie looked up at him, her eyes filling with tears.

"Sunbeam, I didn't give you this to make you cry. I gave you this so you'd remember how strong you and your sisters are."

He sat down beside Winnie, sliding his arm around her and brushing a kiss against her cheek.

"Did you write this?" Winnie motioned to the wood plaque he'd had engraved.

When the sun doesn't shine and the wind doesn't blow, remember you have the light inside you to light your way home.

"I did. I wrote it for you and for all the people who walk through the gym's door taking their first step to standing tall. Winnie, your light is a beacon to me but also to everyone you and your sisters help. You've taken what your parents instilled in you and worked to make the world a better place. I can't imagine how huge your impact will be when all these people you've helped find their light spread it to help others."

Winnie wiped her nose. "This is perfect and I'm going to show exactly how much I love it later when we have time. Your words and this gift are perfect. Do you have an idea where we can hang it in the gym?"

"A couple."

Winnie chuckled. "Of course you do."

"My first suggestion would be by the front door so it's the first thing they see as they come in and the last thing before they leave."

Winnie sniffed again. He wiped a stray tear sliding down her cheek. "No tears. This is a happy day. It's time for my sunbeam to do what she does best and spread her light."

Winnie nodded and brushed a kiss across his cheek above his beard. "Love you."

"Love you, too. Now get a move on and get changed. You can't be late to your own party."

Winnie shook people's hands and kept a smile on her face despite her cheeks aching. She and her sisters had hung her plaque by the front door. All her sisters had loved the plaque but Sarah had understood the underlying meaning. If she knew more about where Bear's head was at, she might be willing to go public. She didn't have that comfort level yet that he wouldn't push her away if something happened to threaten them again.

"Hey, War, I heard you're going to help celebrate the new gym by getting in the ring with Remi again." Cannon's voice carried through the gym.

War rolled his eyes. "Tease all you want. I believe I'm the one with a gorgeous girlfriend, and where's your date tonight?"

"Way to deflect, brother. Are you scared to get in the ring with her?" Flick was always up for teasing.

"War and I don't need to get in the ring. We both know we're evenly matched and I would have had my work cut out for me if he hadn't been incapacitated."

Winnie listened to the banter and knew she'd made the right decision. The teasing was all good and well but not want she wanted Bear to deal with right now.

They were working through being together as a couple and Bear was starting to share more with her, but she knew her man. They were one crisis away from him going to that dark place where he couldn't see any way to keep her safe besides removing himself from her presence.

She wanted it all with him. The beautiful life she'd always imagined. The love she'd watched her parents and Baron and Regina live as an example. When she imagined her fairy tale, she didn't believe it would only be without pain. But life wasn't about not dealing with pain, it was having the person that completed you holding you tight when the storms hit.

"Winchester, you've done good." Locks' arm slipped around her shoulder and he squeezed her into his side. He'd always been there for her and his arm around her shoulder and the smell of gunpowder and wind had gotten her through many a heartbreak during high school. There wasn't a day that her dad didn't shoot his gun either for training or for fun.

"Your mom would love what you've done and how you girls are helping people."

She sniffed and leaned her head against his shoulder. He handed her a handkerchief and then pulled one out for himself, wiping his nose.

"If Mom was here, she'd tell us we could have our moment but then we needed to move on. The world was waiting for us to help make it better."

"Yep. Crying was all well and good but then she'd tell you girls to rub some dirt in it and get back up again."

Her mom had been practical and always reminded them there were things you couldn't change. Take the time to cry over them. If you couldn't change it, then take the first step to change what you could.

"I guess Jesse took her literally since there's rarely a time she doesn't have dirt rubbed somewhere."

Locks' body shook against her as he laughed. "Too true. Each of you girls have some amazing gift. Jesse's is with machines and doing it all while wearing her pink overalls."

Winnie giggled. "Did you hear about the guy that stopped in yesterday because he thought the building was a garage open to the public?"

"No. Unfortunately, I've been banned from your group text."

"Dad, trust me, you should be thankful. We would scar you for life."

Beth walked up, raised Locks' other arm and snuggled in. "What would scar him for life?"

"Our group text."

Beth's pale complexion reddened. "Umm, yeah—just no."

"So tell me about this guy that stopped at the garage. Do I need to visit someone?"

Beth giggled. "Dad doesn't know yet?"

"Girls," Locks growled.

"So, this guy in a Mercedes drives up to the garage. The gate was open for some reason." At the anger blazing in Locks' eyes, Winnie rushed to calm him. "Chill, Dad. Jesse already ripped one of the security guys a new one for leaving the gate open. But back to the story, the guy walks in and Jesse is of course in her pink overalls. And he goes *honey, can you get the guy in charge to come out here,* and you can guess that didn't go over well. She replied *sugar bear, a dick doesn't come pre-equipped with car knowledge. What do you need?* Which should have been his clue that she was the mechanic."

"Okay, my turn, but he didn't. He walks closer to her, puffing his chest out and tells her she better fucking get the real mechanic or he'll make her sorry."

Locks held his finger up at Beth. "I thought you said I didn't need to visit someone."

"Dad, you raised us to stand up to bullies. It gets better. Jesse had been testing the newer bulletproof metal on a stand. She walks over to the gun she was using to test, points it at him, and says, *get off our property or I'll make you sorry.* Then turned and fired multiple times at the metal. She said when she stopped firing she heard his car peeling out. No idea what was wrong with it but he had no problem driving away. She called security and had the person who left the gate open put on grunt duty for two weeks."

Locks chuckled. "I should have known I wouldn't need to do anything but sometimes as a dad, I want to take care of you. No matter how old you grow, you'll always be mine."

Chapter Fifteen

Bear pulled over to the racetrack entrance. He parked his bike behind a tree, then took his helmet off. He opened the backpack he carried and pulled out the night vision goggles. He'd lifted them from the gun range and training center. Hopefully Cannon wouldn't do an equipment inventory before he got them back. He crawled over the fence and started his walk to Winnie's.

She was still wanting them to keep quiet about their relationship. He understood her reasoning but he wanted to let everyone know they were together. He made sure they didn't sit together at Sunday lunch because then he might accidently push her hair behind her ear and kiss her cheek.

He crossed the last fence then paused at the area around the sisters' houses. He pulled the glasses up on his head so he could check the houses. Remi's was dark as was Sarah's. Beth's kitchen light was on and he could see movement in there. Jesse's house had a porchlight on but no lights inside.

His sunshine had her light on in her bedroom but the back door was dark. Her outside light in back was off, too. He slid the glasses back down after texting Winnie he was here. He made his way across. Winnie's door opened and she slipped out.

He pulled her close, tasting her lips which held the faint taste of mint. He pulled back and slid a pair of glasses on her, too.

"Ready?"

"Yes, lead the way."

Holding her hand, he led her back through the field and through the fences. Instead of having her clamber through the last one, he lifted her up over his shoulder and climbed over. When she started to protest, he gave a light slap to her ass.

"Shh. Sound travels at night," he whispered.

Taking her off his shoulder and allowing her to slide down his front made him wish they could just take each other here, but Winnie had wanted a ride. She was helping at the bar tomorrow and wouldn't be riding in the toy run.

He stashed the goggles in his backpack and waited while Winnie got her helmet.

"Can you carry this on your back or do you want me to strap it down?"

"Carry is good. It's a beautiful night for a ride. The sky is clear and the moon is bright. I'm ready to snuggle up with my man."

Bear got on and waited for Winnie to get situated. He started the bike and headed for the road. They were taking paved roads away from the house and the MC compound. Winnie snuggled in behind him, wrapping her arms around him.

With Winnie, he could relax and be himself. He still worried and thought through any scenario but it was different. She not only accepted that part of him but celebrated it. She'd ask his opinion and truly wanted it.

He'd never felt this way about anyone. He loved her and he needed to let her know how much. He'd even driven two and a half hours to Wichita to shop. He'd sworn Scoop to secrecy but he'd wanted someone with him.

They rode for twenty minutes until Bear saw the turnoff. Winnie thought they were just on a ride but he'd planned ahead. He'd bought a camper and dropped it off earlier in the week at Meade State Park. He wanted a night with Winnie where they could be as loud as they wanted and he could lie in a bed beside her.

He planned on setting his alarm for five, which would get her back in plenty of time before anyone was up. He pulled through the entrance and headed toward the campsite. He parked at the RV and waited for Winnie to get off.

"What?" she asked after she took her helmet off.

He took Winnie's hand and unlocked the camper, flipping the light on as they walked in. It had a small booth area, kitchen area, toilet, shower and what he really wanted—a queen-size bed to have Winnie on.

"Did you rent this?"

He shook his head. "Nope, bought it." He hoped it was a good surprise. She turned, taking in the room. Then placed her helmet on the table and unzipped her leather jacket.

"How long do we have?"

He smirked and took off his clothes as Winnie quickly disrobed. "I planned on having us getting up at five so we'd be back before six. If you think that's too late, we'll move it earlier."

Winnie crooked her finger at him, walking toward the bed. "This is perfect, Benton. I'm yours until five. What do you want?"

What a loaded question. What did he want? He wanted it all. This time with Winnie had convinced him they could do this. He wanted the woman, the house, kids, and everyone knowing she was his.

He followed her to the bed. Kneeling on the bed with his ass on his feet, looking at the woman he realized he couldn't live without—he soaked in seeing her nude before him. Her dark hair lying against her shoulders. Her rosy nipples were pebbling and begging him to taste and suck them. Her lean stomach was highlighted by her belly button piercing. Tonight she had in one of the rubber multi-colored ones. He loved the pistol one but it scraped against his stomach last time and Winnie had felt horrible.

Her neatly trimmed hair guarded where he wanted to dive in but he was making this perfect for his sunbeam. He swallowed, took a deep breath and hoped she'd say yes.

"I want you forever. You've taken every cold part of my heart and filled it with your love. I love you and can't imagine not having you in my life. I know you're not ready to share with your family but when you're ready, will you marry me?" He opened the box, showing Winnie the ring he'd found for her.

She sat up from the bed, reaching her hand to touch the ring.

"Benton," her voice was full of tears but she nodded with a wide grin.

He slid the ring on her finger, bringing her hand to his lips. Kissing each individual finger, he knew tonight was the start of their forever. Winnie threw her arms around him, kissing his cheek.

"I love you, Benton. So much."

"I got you this, too. You can wear the ring around your neck on this chain or you can put the ring away until you're ready for everyone to know. You're mine and I can wait as long as you need."

Winnie put the chain on and pressed Benton's chest to get him to lie down.

"I think you might need a reward for being an understanding fiancé."

Her lips claimed his lips, telling him without words how much she loved him, then her hot breath moved on to his chest. He linked his fingers behind his head because feeling her hair trailing against his skin had him wanting to grasp her hair in his hands and direct her, but he was letting her lead. Her tongue slipped out to trace his Bluff Creek Brotherhood tattoo then licked around his nipple. He clenched his abs as his nipples hardened along with his cock. The heat in Winnie's dark brown eyes as she stared at him combined with her fingers ruffling the hair along his abs had him biting his lip, hoping for his control to last.

Her finger rubbed across the head, smearing the liquid on the tip. He fought thrusting up to be closer. *Let Winnie lead.* Then her fingers traced his piercing. He'd been so fucking mad at Roam when he'd gotten it but having Winnie playing with it made all his irritation dissipate. Her touch had him breathing heavier and focusing on curling his toes to keep from coming. Winnie's hand curled around his shaft. His woman felt so good and then she started sliding her hand up and down, tightening it until he couldn't concentrate on anything but Winnie.

He was not blowing in her hand. Her lips nibbled and kissed down the trail of hair on his chest, her hair tickling his side until her hot breath hardened his cock even more. He wasn't blowing in her mouth either, though having her mouth on him with her tongue lashing his piercings had him forgetting why he wasn't. He craved being inside his woman's warm, wet sheath until he couldn't tell where his body ended and hers began.

"Sunbeam, I'm seconds from disgracing myself. Please," he pleaded, pulling his hands from behind his head. He couldn't not touch Winnie so he allowed himself to graze his fingers on her delicate shoulder. He wanted to taste the curve where her neck arched.

"Please sink onto your cock? Please suck you dry? Or please you until you can't remember your name?"

He smirked at his woman's dirty mouth. "I want to come in your hot, wet pussy. I don't care how it happens as long as we both come and I get to feel you shaking around me."

His sunbeam smiled, then swung her leg over his thighs until she was poised above his cock. Her fingers held him upright.

"Right here," she teased him as her wetness barely touched his cock.

He sat up, grasped her waist and started sliding her slowly down his cock. The heat engulfed his head as she opened around him, then her pussy welcomed his shaft. Perfection. "Yes, right here," he whispered as he licked her hardened berry-red nipple and sucked. Winnie squirmed on his cock, intentionally rubbing her clit against his piercing. She'd convinced him to try a ring through it instead of the bar. The first time they'd tried it she'd detonated after a couple of strokes it had felt so good. He'd do anything for his woman, even let her pick his piercing jewelry.

Winnie leaned her head back, moaning. "Oh, that feels good."

She lifted a little then slid back down, encasing his cock in her warmth. He needed to do whatever it took to get her off because he was seconds from blowing. The warning tingle had become a storm.

Heck, Winnie was the only one that destroyed his control just by kissing him. He couldn't allow himself to be swept away tonight. He wasn't screwing up his proposal by misfiring early.

He sucked her nipple a little harder and deeper then pulled away. He moved her hand to the nipple he'd just sucked. "Play with your tit, baby, while I take care of the other."

He waited until she followed his instruction then grasped her poor other neglected nipple between his lips, swirling his tongue around, then slid one hand down to caress her clit. Her breathy sighs and moans had him grinning. He fucking loved the sounds she made. He swirled the wetness around as he continued moving inside her. He pinched then he thrust up farther into Winnie. She tightened as her walls clasped him tight and screamed her climax. Thank fuck.

He thrust one more time then shook, letting ecstasy wash over him. If he could stay right here inside Winnie, he'd be content the rest of his life. He wrapped his arms around Winnie, pulling her close, kissing across her chest. She leaned toward him, letting him take her weight. He lay back down onto the mattress with Winnie's head on his shoulder, his cock still inside her.

"I love you, Benton," she whispered then relaxed against him. He'd already set his alarm on his phone. He should probably clean them up but he didn't want to move her. He had a small hand towel laid beside the bed if she wanted it but for right now, he was content with her in his arms.

He reached over and clicked off the light. Pulling the comforter over them, he relaxed. His sunbeam would be his for everyone to see. As long as he knew they were forever, she didn't have to wear the ring. He just had to have patience and plan for the day when everyone would know she was his. He'd come a long way from the guy who wouldn't commit and could understand Winnie's needs. Someday they'd share what they had with the family but for right now, she was all his.

Chapter Sixteen

B ear took one last look around the new space. Tonight instead of a party at the MC, they were having the diner's grand reopening. It had come together quicker than they'd ever imagined with all the help. Besides two crews from the MC, everyone had given their extra time. He'd never known Scoop was so meticulous about painting and staining. He should have because Scoop had restored his Bronco by himself.

They'd knocked out a cased opening in the front between the two buildings and also a smaller one which allowed a pass-through for staff to easily go between the areas. They'd also added huge windows in the new building, allowing everyone to see the outdoor space the previous owner had used for Saturday fairs and flea markets. The addition of a covered patio with sliding glass walls they could close in the winter expanded the space. Which, since they were reopening two weeks before Christmas, would be used today. A cold front had moved in and his Henley and leather jacket hadn't been warm enough on the way in. By the time he'd ridden the short ride to the diner, he'd been regretting not having a sweatshirt, which he'd texted to Winnie when he let her know he'd gotten there. She'd replied she knew a way to warm him up. He did, too, but with her still wanting to keep it private between them, he wouldn't have a chance to experience any of that tonight at the opening.

The wood floors gleamed with a dark stain and he loved how the rooms flowed into each other. The new building held cases where homemade fudge, candies and pastries could be bought.

He'd talked through his ideas with everyone. They'd jumped on the idea of having some specific motorcycle items to buy along with some other specialty apparel. He'd wanted the diner to become more. A place where motorcycle clubs, travelers and friends could stop, enjoy a meal and relax for a little bit. The upstairs had been redone but he'd left the lights and had the ceiling sealed with varnish to keep the look but minimize the dust. He envisioned it being a place groups could meet and maybe later, he might add books for sale as much as his woman loved them. Having to go to Dodge City or Wichita to buy books was a long ways. When he'd mentioned to Winnie she could just have them delivered, he'd received a lesson in how his woman thought. She read ebooks but she loved the feel and smell of paperbacks. She also wanted to hold them in her hands and browse the aisles for covers that caught her eye.

She'd been gone last weekend with her sisters on a trip to Wichita. They'd all gone shopping for Christmas gifts but had also hit up the bookstores there. Winnie had waxed on about going to the light show at Botanica. Hearing her talk about it had him promising himself that next year, he and Winnie would be doing stuff as a couple and the Christmas lights at Botanica would be one of them.

Regina had left it up to him and the MC members for the name. He'd over thought it but that was his way. His woman didn't disparage his overthinking—she encouraged it. He couldn't explain what having her approval did for him. He'd always despised that part of himself that always saw the what ifs first. Winnie, besides making him fall in love with her, had shown him how to love what he considered the unlovable parts of himself.

He'd made his own trip to Wichita to take care of Winnie's Christmas gift. He'd thought about it and then decided to go with his gut. He only hoped she loved it.

Winnie sipped her drink, enjoying the atmosphere. Bear had crafted the perfect place for everyone to hang out. Watching him accepting the congratulations from their friends and family had her wanting to be right there beside him.

Two weeks ago when she'd had to pretend Bear wasn't the man she loved with all her heart during the toy run, she'd decided they needed to let everyone know about them. Then she'd overheard a conversation about War proposing to Remi at Christmas. She'd decided she'd talk to Bear when they exchanged gifts about going public with their relationship.

Tonight was such a big night for him and she wanted to be sharing in his happiness, not that her man was grinning. His lip would quirk up a little when he was happy but he was still her Bear.

She loved what he'd done with the diner and the look on Regina's face when he'd unveiled the sign for Regina's Roadside Refuge. Seeing Regina pull Bear close and give him a mother's love, which his incubator hadn't ever given him, brought tears to Winnie's eyes.

Winnie had it on her list to sit down with her sisters and discuss his incubator as soon as everyone knew she and Bear were together. Bear had shared late one night how he was worried his biological mom would return and screw things up. When Winnie found out his bio-mom had been extorting money from Bear to stay out of his life for years, she'd been furious.

Bear was one of the strongest, most compassionate protectors she knew but when he talked about his incubator, Winnie could hear the pain in his voice. It made her want to hunt down his incubator and have a little chat. Well, the chat might involve Winnie kicking her ass but it would get Winnie's point across. The diner and him accepting the manager position was a huge step for Bear along with becoming the Vice President of the MC. War had offered the S.A.A. to Cannon and he had accepted. He was putting down roots. With her by his side, they'd figure out what to do if bio-mom threatened Bear or tried to extort money ever again.

Even though the gym had reopened, they'd kept the fight nights to a minimum until after Christmas. The diner remodel and all their other jobs had them stretched thin.

She had an out-of-town security job next week. She was partnered with Scoop and they'd be in Topeka for three days. They'd been partnered for security for a party for some company. It didn't sound like her favorite job but she'd do her part.

Sarah sat down beside her and offered her some of her plate of treats she'd grabbed. "Better grab one if you want the veggie pizza bites, although when they don't have cheese I don't know why they're calling it pizza."

Winnie loved them no matter what they were called and took two pieces of the six before they disappeared. The puff pastry cooked then covered with a mixture of cream cheese, sour cream and ranch seasoning then topped with pieces of carrots, broccoli, tomato and cucumber was a favorite of hers. Bear had asked if she would mind if he used her recipe at the diner and had made her a pan last week. She'd eaten half of it. She would have eaten it all but thought it would be impolite to not share with the man who made it.

The first bite had the flavors bursting on her tongue and her humming in pleasure. He'd used her recipe but it tasted better. Maybe it was because she hadn't done all the work making it.

"Could you keep the sex noises down a little over here? It's just food."

Winnie was taken aback because Sarah usually went out of her way to not say anything that could even be construed as mean.

"Sorry. You know this is my favorite. Everything okay?"

Winnie consumed her two pieces while waiting on Sarah to elaborate. Sarah wiped her mouth and shook her head.

"Yeah. Sorry I'm not my usual self. I just keep thinking that everything was tied up too neatly with the problems we were having. I have that little place on the back of my neck that is itching. It's screaming something is still off."

"I think if you have that feeling then you need to follow it. Mom and Dad both taught us to always follow our hunches. I guess I wanted to believe everything was perfect afterwards. Anything specific you want to talk about or are you still in the processing phase?"

"I appreciate the offer. I don't have enough to start bouncing ideas off anyone yet. I could use a workout, though."

Winnie rubbed her hands together, cackling evilly. "Oh, yes, my pretty—I can make sure your muscles are screaming until you forgot your troubles."

Beth sat down at the table. "Oh no, I recognize that laugh. Who is she going to torture next?"

"I told her I needed a workout. I've spent too much time behind the desk and with the weather, I haven't been running or walking."

Jesse slid in and grabbed a piece of the veggie pizza, finishing it in two bites.

"Hello, sister, did you want to ask before you took my food next time?"

"Whoa, I think someone needs to get laid. You are strung too tight if me grabbing a snack off your plate has you wanting to rip my head off. I know you're not on your period because we're not due until next week."

Sarah rolled her eyes. "You know, some days I love all of you and sometimes I wish I was an only child for just a little while—a week or two."

Winnie decided to be the peacemaker because her sisters were heading toward a knock-down fight, which they hadn't had in forever. It darn well wasn't going to be at her man's new business opening.

"Let's take it down a notch. It's been a busy and wild couple of months. If everyone needs to blow off steam, we can head to the gym after this or you all can calm down and enjoy the evening here."

Beth reached over and palmed the next to last piece of fudge from Sarah's plate. She popped it in her mouth and slowly chewed. Her youngest sister definitely knew how to push Sarah's last nerve.

"Be nice or I'm going to reprogram everything in your house and none of your shows will be available," Sarah threatened.

Winnie decided she wasn't going to play referee anymore tonight. She stood and walked away, dropping her trash, then headed to check out the upstairs. She was curious how he was utilizing the space.

Chapter Seventeen

Scoop was monitoring the cameras around the party and she'd just made her pass through all the areas. The company had their own security, which took care of who was allowed at the party and patrolled the outside.

She and Scoop were in charge of the inside and specifically were on the lookout for anyone trying to leave with the technology the company was showcasing tonight.

The next pass around the party was in fifteen minutes. Scoop would take that one while she watched the cameras and changed her clothes and hairstyle. She started the evening in a ball gown like most of the women attending. Before her next time through she'd pull her hair up into an intricate twist before she changed into a pantsuit.

Scoop would change jackets and put his contacts in. Most people wouldn't give them a second thought, which is what they wanted.

She sat down beside Scoop and took over three of the cameras. Scoop nudged a drink toward her and a plate of snacks.

"I can hear your stomach growling from here."

Winnie wasn't shy about grabbing the snacks and eating. "That's because the food they brought us wasn't enough for the yippy little chihuahua they have. I will never understand the frou frou places that their portions are the size of a quarter to half dollar. I much prefer the food at Regina's Roadside Refuge."

"I bet you prefer the manager there, too."

Winnie waited to see if Scoop would say anything else. Did he know about her and Bear?

"I can hear your brain trying to figure out how to answer me. Yes, I know about you and Bear. I'm very fucking observant and confronted him and basically didn't give him a choice to not share. I'm the only one who knows. The man is gone for you. When he stares at you, the left side of his mouth quirks up and his whole demeanor softens. Grumpy Bear becomes a little less sullen when you're around."

She and Bear hadn't talked about how they would tell people but she hadn't considered someone figuring it out.

"Chill. If you don't want to talk about it, okay, but just know I'm thrilled my friend found his sunshine. You guys are great together."

They were great together because he was everything to her. She'd loved him for so long and when he finally gave in, he'd pushed her away. The only reason she felt comfortable telling him she loved him enough to give him time was because she'd learned so much about him over the years.

"Thanks, Scoop. I'm glad he has you to talk with. I talked with Sarah, too, so you guys both know but no one else yet. Now, you should head out there. You don't want to miss your chance to get hit on."

Scoop laughed and saluted her with two fingers. "It's a jungle out there but I think I can resist."

Winnie moved in front of the screens to keep an eye on what was happening. It had been one of the most boring assignments she'd ever been on but Scoop's words had made it all worth it. It warmed her heart that Scoop could see a difference in Bear because of her. Bear was such a protective, wonderful man and despite his serving in the Army and on the police force, he still didn't see his worth. Maybe by the time they had kids, he would. And they would have kids. Bear was too good with children not to be a father. She'd always imagined herself with six. Some might call her crazy but even when her sisters were driving her to pull her hair out, she loved them and wouldn't trade them for anything.

Six kids sounded like a lot but she had her mother's example to live by. Her mom and dad had always found time to make each of them feel special. From all of them learning to drive Ginger, their metallic green 1970 Monte Carlo, to her parents teaching them all self-defense and how to shoot numerous guns, she'd had an idyllic childhood. Love, laughter and the extended love from all the MC members had her wanting to share it with kids. Winnie didn't even care if she gave birth to them all. With all the children in social services, she wouldn't be opposed to adopting kids. She knew sometimes older kids were passed over for adoptions and it hurt her heart.

She giggled to herself seeing Scoop fending off another woman at the party. Some of the women were being very persistent. She was curious if Scoop found any of them attractive. Since he'd been back home, he had been very circumspect if he was hooking up with anyone, not like Roam, War's brother, and Cannon. Panties dropped all the time around those two.

She kept waiting to see if Regina stepped in regarding Roam. He almost seemed like he was having a midlife crisis because she kept seeing him with different women and he seemed to be drinking more than before. She understood him being upset his wife left their kids but his wife had been a horrible woman and the kids and Roam were better off without her. She'd been gone at least five or six months if Winnie was counting correctly.

Winnie kept an eye on the monitors, thinking about Christmas. She couldn't wait for everyone to open presents. She adored Christmas—the music, the presents, making cookies and candies, and being around her family.

It was going to be a busy week. She offered to help at the diner store to give them some extra hands. The store was exceeding expectations but Bear didn't want to hire anyone outside the MC until they saw sales after Christmas. Of course, if helping at the store gave her a little extra time seeing her man, she'd take it.

Just thinking about him had her smiling. If it took her years, she was going to show Bear how phenomenal he was. Her grumpy guy was going to get the amazing life he deserved if she had anything to say about it.

Chapter Eighteen

If Winnie brushed against him one more time, he didn't care if the whole world found out about them. Her hand sliding across the front of his jeans brushing his cock had him hard in front of all his brothers. He'd been giving her time and he understood why she wanted to keep it secret but he wanted what War had. He wanted to scream at the top of his lungs she was his. Winnie was softening and he wondered if she'd be open to coming clean to the MC after the new year. He wanted to share what they had with the family. He wanted everyone patting his back, letting him know they had his and Winnie's backs.

He'd congratulated the couple and pushed War a little into protecting his territory. He'd collected his money from the originals. His dad and the others were positive they knew War better than he did. He'd known he could win the bet. He slid the money in his pocket and glanced around for Winnie. He wanted to see if he and Winnie could sneak off by themselves.

"Prez, there's a sheriff's car and another car requesting entrance to the clubhouse. They said they need to speak to a Benton Carter."

Bear wondered why a sheriff would be needing him. Although he skirted things now that he wasn't a detective, he hadn't done anything to warrant a chat with the sheriff.

"Let them in. Take the kids to a back bedroom. Any idea what this is about?" War asked.

Bear shook his head, waiting for them to walk in. He had no clue what was going on. The deputy held the door as a woman carrying a baby carrier and holding the hand of small child walked in, followed by another older child. He recognized the dark curls around the cute face he hadn't seen for a while.

"Benton Carter?" the woman questioned. Phoebe saw him and ran toward him, throwing her arms around him.

"Officer Bear, Mommy's gone to Heaven," her words choked off as she started sobbing.

Bear lifted her up, letting her wrap her arms around him. He'd worried about the kids when he'd left the department but he couldn't figure out a way to fix it. He'd even offered Cassidy the option of moving to the MC.

He thought back if he could have done anything different. He and War had met Cassidy when they'd picked her up for soliciting. At first he'd lumped her in with his incubator—a horrible mom. But when he really listened, she'd been a victim of circumstance and had just wanted to feed her kids and make sure they had a place to stay.

He'd been single and very frugal his whole life. He hadn't hesitated picking up groceries and going back over to drop them off. She'd only had two children when he'd gotten to know her. After he'd done some investigating to make sure she wasn't an addict, he'd given her money to pay her rent for a month. He'd also made sure she had his number if she needed anything.

Over the months, he'd fixed a couple things that had broken at her house and given her money for some incidentals. The last time he'd seen her, he'd opened an account for her with nine thousand dollars in it and he'd paid her rent for a year.

When she wasn't interested in coming to the MC, he'd known he had done all he could.

He'd even touched base with her before Thanksgiving and asked if she was okay. He'd also asked if she needed more money. She'd indicated she'd met someone and was pregnant with his baby and due in December. Now he had more questions than answers but none of that mattered. What mattered was how was he going to take care of these kids?

Phoebe's arms were wrapped around his neck and her tears were soaking his shirt. He patted her back.

"Yes, I'm Benton."

"I'm with social services. Cassidy Glickson listed you as the father on all three birth certificates and named you as who the children go to in case of her death. An incident happened and she passed away."

War walked up beside him. "What do you need?"

"I guess I need help figuring out where we're going to stay. What do you need so they stay with me?" Bear questioned, patting Phoebe's back as she continued to cry.

"Although you're listed as the father, I'll need to see where they'll be staying."

Winnie walked up beside him and crouched down beside David. "Hi, I'm Winnie, Bear's fiancée. What's your name?"

The gasps in the room would have probably worried him but right now, the kids needed him and his sunshine was stepping up and letting the world know about them.

"David."

"It's nice to meet you. Are you hungry? I have four sisters and I know one of them would probably love to take you to where the other kids are and get you a snack."

Phoebe pulled her head out of his neck. "I'm hungry. Can I go to?"

Winnie nodded and smiled. "Of course."

In a couple seconds, Beth and Jesse had taken both children into the kitchen. Winnie waited until the door closed then his sunbeam led him toward a table while asking the social worker to join them.

"Now who's this little one and what all do we need to do? Bear hasn't moved in yet to my house but we'd planned to do that in the new year. We hadn't wanted to overshadow my sister's wedding proposal today. With the kids here, we'll be changing that to tonight. Do you need to see it today or do we set up a time later?"

Winnie had the social working eating out of her hand and he was thankful for that. He was stunned. What was he supposed to do? He didn't know how to be a good father and he didn't even get to learn on just one. Suddenly he had three?

"Winnie, thank you for getting the older children out of the room. I was going to ask for privacy. This little one is a boy and he's three days old. We don't have a name for him because Cassidy didn't have a chance to name him. She was attacked in her home and beaten. The assailant left. Neighbors heard the attack and called an ambulance. By the time she arrived at the hospital, the decision was made to remove the baby by cesarean."

"Where were the older kids? Did they see anything?" He worried they would be in danger if they had seen anything.

"They were asleep in their room. Phoebe got up when she heard something and was the one to let the EMTs in. She's refused to speak about anything and I wouldn't allow the police to push a traumatized child."

Winnie had the straps to the carrier unhooked and had the baby snuggled in her arms in seconds. She seemed so comfortable which gave him a little bit of comfort the kids would be okay. "We appreciate that. Now, let's get the business stuff done because we need to get in there and work on making those children understand they're safe."

He glanced at the papers, took the social worker's card and tried to keep his mind in the present and not go into thinking through all the theories. He thanked the social worker and escorted her and the deputy to the door. He and Winnie needed to have everyone start gathering some supplies for the kids.

He knew the owner of the small grocery store in town and was sure he could get them to open up for diapers and formula. He couldn't imagine the small amount in the bag would last long. He turned from the door. Locks was staring at him but his dad was grinning. Baron was smiling beside Rascal.

"What the fuck? You've been dating Winnie, Bear? Did you think you should have given me the courtesy of asking my permission?"

Winnie walked toward Baron, handing him the baby. "Baron, could you please take my son to the kitchen? I don't want him to hear what I'm about to say."

Baron nodded and headed toward the kitchen.

"Bear, you are more than welcome to answer my dad in a moment but I need to say something first."

Winnie paused, waiting on him. His sunbeam fired up was a sight to see and although he wanted to tell Locks what had happened, he wasn't pissing off his fiancée when they'd just become parents to three kids. He nodded because he wasn't sure what he was supposed to say.

"Now, Winnie, this is between Bear and me," Locks protested.

"No, Dad, it's not. Bear and I started dating and I wanted to keep it secret. Growing up, I never got to have anything just for myself. We shared toys, we shared clothes, and we've shared space. I've always had sisters around which I love but for once, I wanted something for myself."

"Winnie, it's not about that. It's about…"

"An archaic notion that as my dad, you get to have final say over who I date? Dad, you raised all of us girls to take over the bail bonds company. You can't have it both ways. You can't raise strong women who can take care of themselves but then shove us back into a box where a man gets to decide whether we can date someone in the MC." Winnie punctuated her point by poking her finger into her dad's chest with each word.

Bear waited for Locks' reply because he wasn't getting between them. Locks and Winnie needed to come to an agreement then he and Locks could talk through their relationship, but it wasn't going to be today. He had three children that needed him.

"Well, fuck, if you didn't sound so much like your mother right then. She'd always tell me when I was acting like an ass. I'm sorry. I still see you as my babies even though you're all grown. I will chat with Bear later. Now, let's get in that kitchen. I'm already going to have to share my grandkids with their other granddad but Baron can fuck off. He's had his own grandkids for a while. It's Rascal's and my turn now."

"Then you need to clean up your words because I'm not having my granddaughter get in trouble at school because of your trash mouth."

Locks shoved Rascal's shoulder. "We both know who has a trash mouth. You'll be the one corrupting our grandkids. I wonder if they have bikes. I should check on that. I'm not above bribing for favorite granddad status."

Winnie's hand grasped his, squeezing lightly as they walked through the door. He could do this. With Winnie by his side and his MC, he could take on the world.

Winnie held Bear's hand as they entered the kitchen and paused at the sight. Beth and Sarah had Grant and David between them. They had snacks out and were running race cars across the top of the bar. Jesse was coloring with Phoebe. Regina sat beside her with one of the twins. Plates of cut up cinnamon roll, and pieces of fruit and toast were beside both kids. Baron was holding the baby which Rascal immediately took from him. Roam was holding Georgia and pouring drinks for everyone. Remington had a phone to her ear and paper and pen in front of her.

"Officer Bear, have you tasted Nana's cinn'mon rolls?"

Bear let go of her hand, walking over to Phoebe. He bent down closer to her. "I have, and did you know she taught me how to make them?"

Phoebe's eyes opened wide. "I want 'em for every meal. Kay?"

Bear brushed her hair away from her face and the frosting smears across her cheeks. "How about we save them for breakfast and maybe special snacks? She has some really good chicken nuggets and macaroni and cheese she makes that is really yummy. I want you to have room for that."

Phoebe nodded and leaned her head toward Bear. "Kay."

"Okay, where are we at? I'm sure you all have accomplished a lot while we were out chatting. My house is larger than Bear's room here so we'll be staying there."

Remington hung up the phone and turned toward her. "Don't think when we get everything organized that we won't be having a little sister chat about keeping stuff from all of us but for now, Jesse and Cannon are going to run over and grab one of the company's SUVs. One of Regina's friends is dropping off car seats. She only uses them when her grandkids visit and they aren't here this week.

"Beth contacted Whiskey because he'd mentioned he'd be visiting someone in Coldwater. He hadn't left Dodge City yet so he's going to buy a variety of formula. Text him which one the baby is currently on. He'll also grab diapers. He said he'd be driving right by here anyway.

"Flick is almost off shift and is grabbing a new parent pack from the firehouse. He said it will have samples of kids' medicine and some other items you might need. Scoop is grabbing a couple guys and moving some of the extra baby and kid items from Regina's house for you to borrow. They have duplicates since Roam moved in with them. Regina's mobilized her posse for kids' clothes."

"We are not a posse. If you're going to call us a group name, I want something cool and hip."

"Mom, I don't think hip is the in word right now," Roam said.

"Here, Mom, let me take Georgia and then you can help organize," War offered.

"Suck up," Roam muttered as he rolled his eyes.

"Can we pause and wonder how Beth had Whiskey's number and knew where he was spending Christmas?" Jesse's teasing voice had Beth glaring at her.

"We'll table that for later. We figure we'll get you set up to get through the next twenty-four hours and then we can make a list of what all you want. I'm always up for a shopping trip and have no problem braving the day after Christmas shoppers in Dodge City or if we need a bigger place, Wichita."

"I'd go with you, Remi, but I'd also babysit if you guys need help," Beth offered.

Winnie walked over to David. He was looking a little scared. She couldn't imagine how they felt. Losing their mom and having a strange person in charge of them. It had taken three days for them to bring the kids to Bear.

Where had the children been during that time? She didn't know but she knew these kids were going to have the best life she and Bear could give them. She and Bear were always going to be together and this just sped it up a little. Her man loved children. She'd watched how he loved on Roam's kids. She'd always wanted a family and these kids needed her.

"David, I might need your help a little," she whispered to him. He had frosting on his lips and was running a car across the bar. He and Grant were crashing them together every so often. Grant would break out giggling and David's mouth would quirk up but he didn't giggle. He didn't have much to giggle about, but she'd help him find his happiness and his sunshine again.

"Why?" he whispered back.

"I need to figure out what toys we need. I also think we might need to figure out maybe a swing set or an outdoor fort. Would you help me make a list of some fun things?"

He turned toward her, tears pooling in his eyes, and wrapped his arms around her neck. She lifted him and cuddled him close, his little body shaking in her arms. She patted his back. She didn't know what to say. His whole little world had been ripped apart. He was scared, missing his mom, and in a new place with people he didn't know besides Bear.

Locks walked over and patted his back. "Hey, buddy, it's okay to cry. I know you miss your mom but your mom knew Bear and his family would love you and take care of you."

His head pulled away from her neck, glancing up at her dad. "You wuv me?"

Locks' grin spread across his face, his teeth bright between his beard. "Of course, I love you. You, your sister and your little brother are my first grandkids. I get to spoil you and play with you. I think Winnie's right. Your house needs a swing set or fort or both. Do you think if I asked nice she might let me help, too?"

David's earnest eyes pleaded with her. "I think we'll let anybody who wants to help because then it will happen faster."

Chapter Nineteen

Winnie snuggled into bed. Bear was checking the house before bed one more time. He'd even doublechecked her smoke alarms were working. By the time they'd moved the kids, some of Bear's stuff, and accepted all the deliveries from different people, she was dead tired.

Luckily she and Bear had changed diapers for Roam's kids so that wasn't something they needed to learn. The kids were bedded down in one of her spare bedrooms which would become someone's bedroom. Her other room had workout equipment in it that had been too heavy to mess with tonight. Tonight had been all about just getting a place for tonight.

Bear walked in. She was exhausted but not too tired to appreciate her man. In deference to the kids in the house, he was wearing gray sweatpants. His wide chest with his tattoo paired with the dusting of hair which arrowed down his stomach had her considering what was more important. Licking down her man's stomach or sleep. Selfishly she wanted to taste every inch of Benton but there was a high chance of them being interrupted tonight. She wanted their door open if the kids needed them.

The social worker had indicated the baby didn't have a schedule yet. Regina had said to expect the baby to wake them every three to four hours if they were lucky. Calling him the baby brought up another point. He deserved a name. She had to push away the emotions about a woman she didn't know dying before she could name her baby or she'd never get through this without turning into a huge puddle of tears.

Bear pulled the cover up and lay down beside her, leaning over to brush a kiss across her forehead. He slid his arm underneath her and tugged her to his shoulder.

"I am petrified. I'm worried I won't be what the kids need. Until I came to live with Rascal, I didn't know moms could be nice. How do I give them what they need?"

His arm tightened and he kissed her forehead again. "You were amazing. You walked over in front of our whole family and claimed me and the kids. I know you wanted to keep it between us for a little longer."

She waited to see if he wanted an answer or still had more to say. Her Benton had so much love to give. He had no idea of his capacity. Tonight, when he'd fed the baby, his hands had been so gentle. She'd heard him quietly singing while the baby finished the bottle. Phoebe and David had crawled up into the chair with him to listen.

"I had my time getting to keep you to myself. Today, I got the greatest Christmas gift. My man and I were given three wonderful children. You asked how you give them what they need? You love them, Benton. Someday, when our kids are grown, you'll look back and see yourself as the man I see. A man whose heart is so full of love it spills over into everything he does. As long as we love them, we'll be fine. I know we'll screw up because my parents freely admit they've messed up. It's not about being perfect. It's about loving so deeply and fully that their lives are overflowing with the joy of being loved. You call me your sunbeam but you completely miss that you're my light. Your care in thinking through situations to keep people safe is your own special light. I love you, Benton Carter, and I'm in this forever. I'll ride with you forever in this life."

A sniff and a shudder working through his chest heralded Benton pulling her tighter.

"Are you sure I can do this?"

Benton's stoic face most days presented an unfeeling visage to the world but his quavering voice illuminated how much her man felt.

"Yes, I know we can do this together."

"Love you," he whispered.

Chapter Twenty

Bear stirred as he heard a faint cry. He worked to untangle himself from the arms and legs of Phoebe and David. They'd come in to join them around three. He was guessing the cries of the baby had woken them and they'd been scared in a new place.

Winnie had helped them get situated between the two of them. It hadn't taken any time and they'd both gone back to sleep. Phoebe had whispered as she snuggled in that they could always go to their mommy's bed when they were scared.

He had no problem doing whatever was needed to make the kids feel secure but he was ordering a king-size bed. Winnie's queen was a little too crowded. He'd woken up once because David's foot had hit his crotch as Phoebe's legs pushed him away from her.

He grabbed the monitor. It was six a.m. so he might as well get up. He'd let Winnie and the kids sleep. She'd gotten up at four and at five. Regina's timeline of the baby waking every two to three hours had been a pipe dream. They'd been up every hour and had been up for about twenty minutes each time.

He had a list of questions for Regina because he wanted to make sure he wasn't doing something wrong.

He lifted the baby out of the bassinet and cuddled him close as he got the items ready. Rascal had wasted no time informing him to keep his little buddy covered if he didn't want peed on. Of course, then Rascal had to share how Bear had peed on him.

Bear laid the baby down and quickly had him changed into a new diaper and a new onesie. He'd leaked through his diaper a little. He grasped him under the butt and held the back of his head as he carried him out to the kitchen. He flipped on a light and swayed as the baby started to whimper.

"I've got you, bud. Give me a second to heat this up." He slid the premade bottle into the warmer, humming as he swayed to keep the baby from crying louder. "Let's keep this down so your siblings and Winnie can sleep."

He loved Winnie before this had happened but he had no idea his capacity for love until these little ones had walked into his life. When Winnie had walked over and claimed them all, he'd known he'd fight to keep his family together.

The light came on so he knew the bottle was ready. He was thankful they were able to borrow so much from Regina and Baron. At least he couldn't screw up heating up the bottle.

He and the baby headed into Winnie's front room. No, his and Winnie's front room. He started to sit when he heard a light tapping on the front window. He pulled back the curtain. Rascal and Locks were smiling on the front porch, motioning to be let in.

He unlocked the door and motioned them in. Locks carried an insulated coffee carafe and Rascal had a box of bakery items. They walked into the kitchen, dropping their items on the island, then washing their hands in the sink.

Rascal held his hands out for baby. "I won the toss so I get to feed him his bottle. Locks gets the next time."

Rascal settled in the recliner with the baby in his arms, motioning Bear back to the kitchen.

Locks had a cup of coffee and was sitting at the island sipping it. "Bear, feel free to go back to bed or grab some breakfast. Once all the guys get here, we'll get the spare bedrooms cleaned out. The swing set supplies are scheduled to get here at noon. Regina is supplying all the meals for everyone helping today."

Bear was wide awake so he poured himself a cup of coffee and checked the box. Rascal had gotten a variety. He selected a blueberry cake donut and a twist.

"Were you and Rascal waiting at your house for the lights to come on?"

Locks grinned. "I offered for him to stay the night in the main house. I knew he wouldn't want to be far from you just like I didn't want to be. We're both early risers so I made coffee and he ran to the diner to grab some breakfast for everyone. How'd the kids do?"

"We put them in their own room like Regina suggested but they came into ours around three. We need a king-size bed."

Noah nodded, taking another sip of his coffee. "If you're good with it, we're going to have the spare bedrooms emptied and the items stored in the smaller garage. Since I've got two girls who've already found men, I think we need a place to store furniture as households are combined. Then as we add new staff or help survivors get a new start, we could offer them some furniture. I know Winnie will want to keep the workout equipment from the fourth bedroom. We'll see where she wants to set it up but it can be stored in the garage for now. We've got king beds in all the rooms at the main house. Why don't we switch one out today so you have more room?"

Bear loved his MC family and today was just one example of how problems were solved by everyone helping each other. For the first time since he'd found out about the kids, his shoulders relaxed a little. He wasn't naïve enough to believe there wouldn't be problems along the way but he and Winnie were surrounded by the best family.

Cassidy would have been a good mom and his heart ached for the baby never knowing how much Cassidy loved him. David might or might not remember her.

Cassidy had been nothing like his incubator. She'd fought to keep her kids safe and she just needed a little help. He'd been in a position to provide it. Now that he was past the shock of becoming a father to three, he'd need to have Scoop look into what had happened. The social worker had mentioned an incident but hadn't elaborated. He needed to know exactly what had happened and if his kids were in danger.

Rascal walked back in. "I burped him. He's all yours, old man."

Noah eagerly reached for the baby and cuddled him next to his shoulder. "I'll head in and we'll cuddle for a nap." Noah paused when the baby grunted then the sound of him filling his diaper echoed in the kitchen. "Seriously, is this what type of grandpa you're going to be?"

Bear watched to see how his dad would respond to Noah's manipulation.

"Quit being whiney. If he'd filled his diaper before I brought him back, I would have taken care of him. He was in your arms when it happened so act like an adult and take care of him. I don't want a whiney fucking grandparent as my co-grandparent."

Winnie woke to little hands patting her face lightly. Cracking open her eyes, Phoebe and David were leaning over her face, their noses almost touching hers.

"Officer Bear's not here. He didn't leave us, did he?"

She sat up, pulling the kids closer for a hug. "Good morning. I don't see the monitor so I'm sure he's up with your baby brother. Bear and I won't be leaving you. We love you and you're ours. Now, we might be gone at different times because we both have work but you'll always be with somebody in the family who loves you. I'm hungry. Shall we go potty and then see about some breakfast?"

Winnie quickly had the kids through the morning routine. Phoebe was holding her hand tightly and David had wanted her to carry him. It would most likely take a long time for them to understand this was home. She paused in the doorway at Locks and Rascal disagreeing in the kitchen.

"Oh, you said a bad word." Phoebe turned to Bear. "Are you going to put him in timeout?"

Bear smiled at her. Her man freaking smiled and leaned down close.

"I don't know how timeout will work with him."

"You know, we may be fine but we can always use college money. How about a swear jar for you guys?" Winnie grinned at Rascal's smirk. He pulled his wallet out and pulled out five twenties.

"That should cover me for a couple weeks."

Phoebe walked closer to the money, her finger running across the closest bill. She turned back to Winnie with wide open eyes.

"I think we should keep track. I think he's going to say a lot of bad words. We don't want to miss out on any."

Bear picked her up. "That's an excellent idea. How about a doughnut for breakfast?"

Winnie helped David get situated and let him pick his doughnut. She leaned closer to Bear. Brushing a kiss across his lips, his beard rubbed against her face.

"When did the grands get here?"

His arm slipped around her shoulders, brushing a kiss against her cheek while keeping an eye on the kids.

"They showed up when I flipped the light on to give the baby his bottle. They've got our whole day planned, including cleaning out bedrooms."

Winnie filled a cup of coffee, giggling at her dad's glare at Rascal when he came in with a freshly changed baby. Which brought up an issue—the baby needed a name. She didn't want to upset the kids but if their mom had already picked a name, she wanted to honor that. There wasn't an easy way to ask so she might as well just throw it out there.

"I think we need something else to call your baby brother. Had your mom said a name you were going to call him?"

Phoebe shook her head no.

"Okay, then it's up to us. I'm thinking we start making a list and then think through what sounds right. I bet one of my sisters has some posterboard we can use."

David took a huge bite of doughnut then answered. "Wike Fred."

She had no clue what he'd said but maybe when he was done they could figure it out. She heard honking along with the rumble of multiple motorcycles.

"Looks like our help is here."

Locks handed off the baby and he, Rascal, and Bear headed outside. She picked up her phone and texted her sisters.

Winnie: If anyone is up, I need backup. Testosterone overload with the males thinking I should be the only one staying with the kids, apparently.

Jesse: On my way. Just got some modifications done to a side by side for you.

Sarah: My pumpkin bread and banana bread has a couple more minutes in the oven. I'll be over as soon as it's out unless you need me to kick someone's ass before then.

Winnie: I'll wait for fresh pumpkin bread. Did you make honey butter?

Sarah: Seriously? You have to ask. I made a huge amount for the invasion.

Winnie: Am I the only one who doesn't know what is happening today?

Remington: Since you had the kids, we didn't include you in the planning texts. You should thank us, seriously, it's good we have unlimited texts. The MC put out the call for help. You have Whiskey and his whole family along with all the MC plus some people from town. Regina and Sarah are coordinating food.

Beth: I coordinated toys and kids beds. I ordered a couple options for comforter colors and will return what we don't need. One of Whiskey's brothers is picking up our order once the store opens. He was visiting in Wichita so he won't be here until after lunch. If you think of something before ten, let me know and I'll have him grab it.

Jesse: I know you have a certain way you like stuff, everything being done can be changed later. Everyone wanted to take care of immediate needs. Sarah added a form where people can sign up to help you guys including doing early morning feedings so you all can sleep. She had to add where one person couldn't fill out all the spots because Rascal and Dad were fighting over them all.

Winnie: They were fighting over who had to change a dirty diaper when I came out.

Remi: I foresee a lot of competition between Rascal and Dad. I bet all the kids end up with mini motorcycles, regular bikes and more toys than they'll ever need. You might need a bigger house or a larger garage just for the toys.

Beth: We're giving you a week then we'll be doing a girls' night so you can tell us all about your and Bear's courtship.

Winnie: Courtship?

Beth: I'd considered clandestine fucking but thought you might take offense to that.

Jesse: I agree with clandestine. How the hell you kept it from us is amazing.

Winnie: Gotta go. The kids need me.

Remington: Chicken.

Beth: Bac Bac Bac

Jesse: You can run but you can't hide. We know where you live.

Sarah: Bread is out. Jesse, can you pick me up? I could use some help.

"Okay, kiddos, let's go get dressed so we can do all the fun stuff."

She helped the kids wash hands, brush teeth, and do all the things to get them ready. Phoebe was a helper. She not only tied her own shoes but helped her younger brother. Once everyone was dressed, she checked the bag for jackets or coats. There was one light jacket but nothing substantial. She'd checked the temperature and it was in the sixties with a breeze.

She laid the baby on the bed with a pillow on either side of him, more for protection from his siblings since he was too young to roll over. She dug through her zippered sweatshirts. She was sure she had a couple size smalls she hadn't given away yet.

She found two. "Okay, these might be big but will keep you warm until we can get you some other ones."

"Anybody here?" Regina called.

"In here."

Regina appeared in the doorway with a bag. "Oh, looks like I'm just in time. I brought some of Grant's clothes for David. A couple women from town dropped off a bag for Phoebe. I pulled out the jackets."

Regina walked over with a pretty purple jacket with sparkly buttons. "Do you remember me from yesterday? I saw this and thought it would look so pretty on you."

Phoebe nodded and let Regina slip the coat on her. Then Phoebe swirled around, dancing in her new coat, her eyes shining brightly and a smile on her face.

"I also brought snacks and food for lunch. Let me get that in and then I can watch the baby while you and the younger ones give your opinion on where you want the play area."

Winnie was thankful for Regina's suggestion. She loved the guys but if they were adding a play area, which sounded like it was more than a swing set, she wanted to have a say.

Chapter Twenty-One

Winnie stood with her sisters in the front room watching the guys work. Bear in jeans and a flannel looked amazing. Add in the Franks and Daughters ball cap on backwards and he was droolworthy. Their relationship was finally out in the open but she still couldn't steal her man away for some alone time because they'd been invaded, in a good way. What was it about a ball cap on backwards that made her want to kiss her man?

"Don't you wish it was a hundred degrees out? Can you imagine this view only without shirts?" Beth mentioned.

Phoebe tugged on her hand to get Winnie's attention, her forehead scrunched with the cutest questioning look. "Why no shirts?"

Winnie bit her lip, letting her youngest sister figure out how to answer that question because she was starting out as she intended to go. Her siblings would have to learn to watch what they said around the kids.

"Umm, because then it would be easier for the guys to move the wood. Their bulky jackets are slowing them down but umm, since it's cold they have to wear them. I think they'd be so much faster without them."

Winnie kept her giggle in but Beth's eyes pleading for help from all of them was hysterical. All of them waited to see what Phoebe would say.

"I want my swing set right away. I'm going to go ask Bear to tell them all to take off the coats."

Although Winnie had no problem throwing Beth under the bus when it was to her advantage, she was stopping this.

"How…"

"Oh my goodness, Phoebe. I need some help rolling out this cookie dough I brought. Could you and David help me?" Regina held out her hands until the two kids followed her. She winked and mouthed you're welcome to them.

Beth waited until the kids couldn't hear and then giggled. "Oh crap, besides curbing my cussing, now I have to think about everything I say regarding the sexiness of the guys. Drooling over the guys is one of my favorite pastimes."

"Mine, too." Jesse fanned her face as she motioned outside.

"Have you seen the thighs and ass on Scoop? For sitting at a computer all day, Rocky Road has one you could bounce a quarter off of," Sarah said.

"You all can drool all you want. My man is by far the most droolworthy." Remington sighed.

"You mean once he pulled his head out of his ass?" Beth whispered.

Winnie shook her head. "Good try. A whispered cuss word still means you pay. You, too, Sarah."

"What the hell? How is ass a cuss word? I mean are you going to charge me if I say jack ass meaning a mule? I mean I totally understand about fuck, shit, damn, asshole and fucking asshole because you don't want the kids saying it when they go to school, but I think we need a ruling. I work in an office with computers, computer programs, and people that sometimes need their asses kicked."

"So, if we do fifty cents a cuss word, by my calculations you owe the swear jar five dollars and fifty cents. If we do a dollar, fork over eleven dollars, sis." Jesse held out her hand, waggling her fingers at her sister with a grin on her face.

Winnie stared at her usually calm sister. She wasn't sure what was going on with Sarah but she was sure she'd find out when her sister was ready.

"Since we could hear all those from the kitchen, Phoebe said you should probably bring a lot of money because she said you have a potty mouth. I vote for a dollar and maybe keep track of the worst offenders with them getting an extra fine at the end of the month."

Winnie snorted, then couldn't hold her laughter in. Remington laughed so hard she bent over. Jesse laughed until tears came out her eyes. Beth laughed but shook her finger at Sarah.

"Listen, chick, as the youngest, I've dealt with you guys always being better than me. Remington shoots the best. Sarah bakes the best. Winnie fights the best and runs the fastest. Jesse can fix anything mechanical under the sun and still look cute doing it in her pink coveralls. If you think I'm giving up the title of most inventive cusser, think again." Beth punctuated each item by poking her finger in each sister's chest.

"I think you're good at a lot of things, Beth. Heck, on surveillance you change your appearance like a chameleon and sometimes even I can't recognize you." Winnie pulled Beth close, leaning her head against her sister's. "And honestly, without you all I wouldn't have survived the first eighteen hours with the kids."

Watching the squabbling and ribbing between her sisters gave her a sense of peace. Her kids would grow up with a family who knew how to love but also disagree. She and Bear may have just started out on this journey with the kids together but she had no doubts they would make a loving home for the kids. Now if they could figure out what to name the baby.

Bear held the board as Whiskey nailed the pieces together. Bear was grateful Whiskey and his brothers and cousins had helped. They were almost finished with the fort that the kids climbed up into to slide down.

Even though the sisters' houses were separated from the bail bonds building by a gate, he'd wanted something more when they realized in front of the houses was the best place for the playground.

Rascal and Locks were currently working with Whiskey's brother, Hennessey, and Gage on how best to install it but still have it look good. Rascal and Gage were currently in a standoff because even though Gage was in charge of their Texas chapter's building company, Rascal was positive he knew better. His latest comment showed exactly why Gage had gone to the other chapter to prospect. Bear's dad throwing in he'd changed Gage's diapers and Gage better listen to him had escalated the conversation to a yelling match.

Bear stepped in to push his dad back from Gage.

"How about you let me do my job? When I'm getting a tattoo, I'll listen to you," Gabe muttered as he backed away.

"I'll have you know these are my grandkids and I want them safe."

"Rascal, I do, too, but there are ways we need to build the barrier. Just digging a hole today when we haven't figured out how big or how wide could make us have to re-do something."

Rascal relaxed and shook his head. "Anyone ever tell you how much you guys piss me off when you talk sense and I have to give in?"

Gage laughed. "No, but you owe money to the swear jar."

"I'm going inside to see the kids and get some coffee and pay into the swear jar."

Bear glanced around, checking their progress. It had been a long day but they were getting ready to knock off for supper. He'd smelled chili, vegetable soup and homemade bread when he'd walked through earlier. Some of the guys had grabbed extra tables and chairs and set them up in the living room. It was a good thing the house was an open concept because they had over forty people to feed tonight.

War walked up to the door as Bear opened it.

"How's it feel, Dad?"

Bear slapped his friend on the back. "Pretty awesome except I'm ready for Locks and Rascal to go home. They came before six and I'm ready for a little peace."

War laughed and shook his head. "I think you're tough out of luck. I heard Rascal asking if he could stay over at Locks' again tonight so they could come do one of the nighttime feedings."

Not what he wanted but seeing his dad holding the baby and smiling was worth any annoyances he felt. He had a family when he never thought he would so he'd take his dad being around.

Chapter Twenty-Two

Bear lay beside Winnie listening to her breathe deeply. He should be sleeping because the baby would be up in a couple hours but he couldn't. In the last three days since the kids had come to live with them, he'd had zero alone time. Someone was always around and the list for taking care of the kids with the additional dishes and laundry was endless.

He needed a second to himself. He gingerly moved Winnie's head off his shoulder, sliding a pillow underneath her. Her breathing stayed the same so he headed out to the kitchen, grabbing his reading glasses off the dresser. He didn't need them very often but if he messed up a stitch and needed to fix it, he would. Plus he was turning on the bare minimum of lights. In fact, he'd use one of the rocker recliners in the breakfast nook area. Winnie had rearranged the house to make it easier for people to help with the kids. She'd originally had a treadmill and a separate TV near the fireplace area off the kitchen. When the guys had moved it out, she'd replaced it with two plush rocking recliners along with a large rug to make the stained cement floor a warm place for the kids to play.

He opened the closet to the left of the fireplace and grabbed his basket on the top shelf. The guys had brought his crochet supplies over when they'd moved all his stuff. He hadn't had a free moment but crocheting always helped him focus his thoughts.

He settled in the recliner with the small light turned on beside him. He'd finished Regina's blanket two weeks before Christmas and hadn't been able to wait to give it to her. He'd crocheted a chevron pattern using the colors in her front room. When he'd delivered it to her house, she'd hugged him, cried, then hugged him some more. He was glad he could try to show her how much she meant to him.

After Regina's, he'd started a blanket with a variegated yarn of blue. He hadn't had a purpose for the blanket but he did now. He'd finish this as a small one for David then buy some variegated yarn in pink for Phoebe. Jesse had worn her pink overalls over the first day she'd dropped off the modified side by side and Phoebe couldn't quit talking about how cute they were.

He chuckled quietly to himself. Looked like he was a girl dad and if she loved pink, then he would, too.

He worried, though, if he'd be a good enough dad. What if when the kids upset him, he started acting like his incubator did? Would he lock them in a room without food or heat? What if he snapped at some point and slapped them across the face like she'd done? He shivered thinking back over the times he could remember before Rascal rescued him. He knew people said little kids didn't remember things but he had vivid memories of the things she'd done. At times, his dreams were vivid and he was back in that cold, dirty house with the woman who would rather hurt him than hug him. He didn't remember any time she'd ever been kind to him.

What if she returned and tried to hurt the kids? He had so much anger toward her and the things she'd done to him as a child and as an adult. She might have birthed him but he wasn't letting her anywhere near the kids. He slowed his breathing down when he realized his hand was clenching the crochet hook and he was shaking. As mad as he was at her, he knew he'd do everything in his power to keep them safe. He realized he'd rather kill himself than ever hurt them. Maybe Winnie was right and he should talk with a professional about his childhood. She'd mentioned she and her sisters had all gone to counseling after they lost their mom to deal with their grief. Winnie didn't see it as weak. She'd reminded him it took a strong person to open their hand and reach for help. Maybe it was time to take the steps to heal from the past.

He turned back to the blanket and started crocheting again. The kids and Winnie deserved the best version of himself he could give them. Since he'd fallen in love with Winnie, he'd worried he'd be enough for her then they'd gotten the kids. Winnie grounded him and the peace he felt with her was indescribable. He wanted to make sure he was giving her the same back. He'd never be perfect but he could be enough for her and the kids. He'd take his hard days and share them with someone who could help him put them in perspective. He'd work on the blanket for a little bit but he was positive he had a plan that would help his family.

A creak had him turning toward the bedrooms. Phoebe stood there, sucking on her thumb, her brown curly hair pulled in front of her face.

"You okay, Phoebe? Couldn't sleep?"

She nodded, keeping her head down. He laid the blanket and hook down, pushed the recliner down and walked slowly toward her. Bending down on one knee, he heard a creak from his knee. If he was going to keep up with three kids, he might need to take Winnie's advice to do yoga, but he'd worry about that later. He put his hand lightly on Phoebe's shoulder.

"Do you want to cuddle in the recliner or do you want me to come back and lie on the floor by your bed?" Tonight wasn't the first night she'd woken up.

"Can we cuddle in the recliner and will you sing to me?"

He'd stumbled through singing a song to her last night before bed. She'd asked him to sing to her and he'd croaked out whatever she wanted as long as it brought a smile to her face with her dimple.

He settled into the recliner, leaning it back, and covered her with the quilt Winnie had in the basket. She moved around until she had her head exactly where she wanted and her cold feet tucked in. He wrapped one arm around her and held the quilt tighter around her feet.

"What song? Did your mom sing to you?"

Last night had been a couple of pop songs which Winnie had to help him with and a couple kid songs. He wondered what she'd ask for tonight. Winnie and he had discussed they weren't acting like their mom had never existed. Cassidy had done what she could for them and deserved to have her memory kept alive.

"She sang 'Hard Days' or 'Here Comes The Sun.'"

Winnie loved country and so did a couple of his brothers so he knew Brantley Gilbert's "Hard Days."

He started singing softly, trying not to wake anyone else. Phoebe hummed along with him for a little bit then her head got heavier along with her breathing. The words hit him right in the heart. He'd gone through some hard days but he had the chance with these perfect little children to make sure he lightened their days as much as he could. He sang the last couple words, waiting to see if she was really asleep. Maybe they'd stay here just a little longer. He switched off the light. He'd move her back to her bed in a minute. Right now, he was going to cuddle his girl and keep all the bad dreams away, for both of them.

Chapter Twenty-Three

Bear was working in the diner this morning. He had to sign paychecks and oversee their ordering. Although he had capable people working for him, he still needed to make sure everything was perfect. Regina trusted him and he wasn't letting her down.

They'd had the kids a week and had finally gotten into a rhythm. Despite he and Winnie wanting to do things on their own, there was no saying no to their dads. At least they'd convinced them to only come in the early mornings.

He and Winnie were able to sleep in until seven, which was a blessing. Rascal or Locks was taking the five a.m. feeding. They'd use their key to get in, feed Joey and then put him back down. Joey was now sleeping at least two hours between feedings and sometimes longer.

He smiled thinking of Phoebe's disgust with the voting for the name. She and David had come in and said they didn't like any of the top three names. He and Winnie had asked them which ones they liked. They both said the same name. Winnie had looked at him and said well, you're the siblings so you get extra votes. Let's tell Joey his new name.

Later that same evening, Winnie's sisters had invaded and decided they needed to do a dance party. When the *Friends* them song came on, Phoebe started singing along and knew all the words.

Beth had asked her how she knew the song. Phoebe had looked at her like she was stupid then said, "It was Mommy's favorite song, silly. That's who I'm named after," then the name the kids had chosen made perfect sense. They'd all had a good laugh that no one had realized Phoebe Lisa and David Ross were from the show. Even though there were numerous Matts in the MC, they had to name the baby Joseph Matthew. His crazy woman and her sisters had more in common with the children than he'd ever known.

The temperature had dropped and snow was forecasted late tonight or early tomorrow morning. Beth, Sarah, Jesse, and Winnie had driven to Wichita to grab essentials for the kids and their house. All the stuff from their friends was nice but Winnie and he both wanted the kids to get to play in the snow which meant snowsuits, heavy gloves and snow boots. Plus, Winnie had a running list of all the things she'd noticed the kids needed. They'd taken one of the SUVs so they'd have plenty of room to bring stuff back.

Remington and Rascal were on kid duty until he got back home. He was going to spend a little time planning some meals for them. The stuff everyone had dropped off was great but he'd been chatting with the kids, finding out their favorite foods. He'd found a recipe for homemade mac and cheese that he wanted to try. The kids raved about their mom's mac and cheese and when listening to them describe it, he thought he might have figured out the recipe.

They also talked about her making her own pizza crusts and them getting to make their own pizzas. He had a crust recipe and was going to make sure he had all the toppings. He was guessing at how much they'd need because so far someone had always dropped in for either lunch or supper with them. He'd been a little crabby about it at first until he'd realized how the kids loved having family around.

Phoebe had asked about Grandpa Rascal or Grandpa Locks reading a bedtime story to them. He'd sent a text out and had one of them scheduled for tonight and the other for tomorrow night. He couldn't bring their mom back but he was going to be the best dad for them. They would never want for anything, especially affection and love.

He finished the paychecks, checked over their sales for the last week and was pleasantly surprised with how much apparel had sold. He'd known the food items would fly off the shelves. They were currently keeping their production the same because with it being the week after Christmas, he expected the candy items might drop off because of people switching out of holiday mode.

He scrutinized the shop area as he entered. Everything was clean, orderly and ready for the next shopper to fall in love with something. Scoop was in the shop area. He notified them all he was upgrading the security at all their businesses. Bear had given up trying to keep up with all the modifications. He was thankful his brother was protecting their business.

"Hey, Scoop, how's the upgrade going?"

"Good. I took the morning shift because I worried about anyone trying to check out people while I was upgrading. I'll add the sale in manually before I leave today."

"Thanks." Bear checked the racks and then the extra storage area behind. It looked like the numbers were correct. They had sold a huge amount of clothing.

"Have you sold any clothing this morning? I've been off for a few days and our clothing sales are significantly higher than I projected."

Scoop laughed and nodded. "Oh yeah, you need to reorder. They have a list here of items people wanted and were out of stock. It looks like the sweatshirts you ordered as a joke for the sisters were put out for sale. There's a list here of fifty people who want you to order them one. You also have a list of like forty people wanting the property of keychains with our logo. By the way, I'm completely okay with that, but some chick this morning pointed at my name on my cut and asked me if she could get one with Property of Scoop on it. Um, no way! I don't care how much they'll pay."

"You're kidding, right? About her wanting one with your name on it?"

Scoop clicked a couple of other keys, then shook his head. "I wish I was."

Bear patted Scoop's shoulder. "Hang in there. At least she wasn't trying to get a property of cut with your name on it."

Scoop shuddered. "Don't you even joke about that. So, Dad, how's it feel now that your relationship is out in the open and you suddenly have an instant family?"

"Like it's the best thing that's ever happened to me. Almost like a dream because it's too good to be true. I keep waiting for it to all go to crap."

Scoop nodded and knocked on the table. "We've got your back, brother. Enjoy the ride but know I'm diving into everything I can about the situation."

"Thanks, Scoop."

Scoop's encouragement meant the world but it didn't mean he wasn't still concerned.

Winnie grabbed a cart while Jesse grabbed one, too. "Okay, Sarah, you and Jesse have your list. Beth and I will do ours. Let's try to keep this store to an hour and a half max. If they don't have something in stock, circle it, and feel free to add anything to your list. These kids have done without. If you see something cute, grab it. Beth and I are starting in the baby area. If we finish first, we'll join you in the next area."

"10-4, M-I-C," her sisters answered in unison.

"What is M-I-C?"

The grins on her sisters' faces told her they were enjoying this entirely too much.

"Mom in charge. We thought it had a nice ring to it." Beth couldn't even keep a straight face through the explanation before she started giggling.

"Cute. Now time's a wasting. Get going."

Winnie grinned at her sisters but then saw the cutest little baby outfit with a motorcycle on it. She grabbed a couple in different sizes. She'd spoiled Roam's kids but having her own was completely different. She wasn't denying herself or the kids anything today.

Beth brought over a couple infant snowsuits along with hats and mittens and a large pile of blankets.

"That's a lot of blankets." Not that she cared how many blankets but there were six identical blankets.

"We didn't get hardly anything from the kids' house. When I asked the social worker, she said there had been a break in and a lot of the kids' things were destroyed. I was going to tell you guys later after we got back but since you asked about the blankets, I'm getting each of the kids two. One main blanket to cuddle with and a replacement. I texted Remington to ask her if the kids had any loveys they missed. I'm going to look for them next and make sure they all have duplicates. These kids are not losing everything because someone decided to hurt their mom." Beth's voice broke as she explained and brought tears to Winnie's eyes. Winnie slid her arm around her sister.

"You are the best. I love you so much and love you even more because you love my kids."

Beth sniffed, wiped her face, and dropped the items in the cart. "We have stuff to do and don't have time for a Code Rachel. We can meet some other time and cry to our hearts' content."

Beth headed over to the area for David and Winnie got back to shopping for Joey. She found multiple shoes she loved and tossed them in. She also grabbed a couple replacement pacifiers. Sometimes it was the only thing that helped calm him down.

She saw a jean jacket that was too cute. She tossed a couple in. Maybe Sarah could embroider the club's patch on one for him. She couldn't have him be the only one with a Bluff Creek Brotherhood MC patch jean jacket.

Winnie: See if there are jean jackets in Phoebe and David's sizes. Grab a couple. Could you embroider the MC patch on them Sarah? I think Bear would love it.

Jesse: They have dark denim but also a black one. Do you want a couple of each for Phoebe in her size and one up?

Sarah: Yes, that would be fun. See if there are any ball caps in the kids' size. I could do the bail bonds patch on caps for them. You better grab extra because if Bear's kids have them then you know Roam's kids will want them too.

Beth: I grabbed a couple for David. We might need another cart. I'm going to grab one.

Winnie: TY

Winnie turned around to see if there was a black one in Joey's size, too, almost running into a woman standing in her way.

"Excuse me." Winnie waited for the woman to let her by. She catalogued her features. A little shorter than Winnie so under six foot. Blonde hair with a hint of darker roots. Her face had some wrinkles indicating she wasn't young, and thin with a light layer of well applied makeup. Her designer bag with slacks and blouse told Winnie she either had money or bought the items at a high-end resale shop. The woman looked Winnie up and down then stepped closer, reaching toward Winnie's arm.

"I need you to deliver a message."

"I don't know who you are or what message you have but you need to step back and not touch me. Who are you and what do you want?"

Beth had paused with her cart and moved behind a rack, perusing it as if she wasn't with Winnie.

"My, he found a feisty one with you. I need you to tell Bear I know where he is and I'll be by to pick up what he owes me."

"Well if I know a Bear, who would I say is dropping by?"

The woman chuckled. "Oh, you're quite the chip off the old block and I don't mean that in a good way. He'll know.

Now do as I say. You don't want to know what happens when I don't get my way."

The woman turned and walked toward the exit. Winnie signed the ASL letter F which was their hand signal for follow.

Winnie: Code Phoebe. Jesse follow Beth outside. Sarah baby section.

Winnie thought she'd just met Bear's mom and she wasn't impressed. She had to wonder how the woman had found them in the store. Besides her family, no one knew they were shopping in Wichita today and they didn't even know which stores they were going to.

Sarah walked up and wrapped an arm around Winnie's shoulder. The warmth of her sister's arm made her realize how the woman's words had chilled her to her core.

"You okay?" Sarah whispered while keeping an eye on their area.

"I will be but if that's who I think it is, she has no idea what I'll do to keep the kids safe."

Beth returned with Jesse by her side. "I got pictures of her and was able to get the license plate and make and model of the car. She got in by herself and drove herself away. She headed south which would take her to the light where she could be going anywhere. I think we need to finish our shopping here then pick up the SUV. Then Jesse and I can drop back a little and see if we have a tail. I honestly wasn't looking for one when we came here today."

"SUV?" Winnie questioned.

"Dad wants you to have one of the armor-plated SUVs for his grandkids. I'm picking up a new one to modify and replace the one you're getting. I agree with Beth. My neck is itching. We need to enjoy shopping today but be careful. Now the question is, how do you want to handle this? Do we send the info to Scoop and let him start working on it? You'll need to let your man know because he'll go ballistic if Scoop knows something about you that he doesn't, or do we wait until we get back and let Sarah dig in?"

Winnie sighed, trying to figure out what was best. "I don't know. I can see the benefits of both. Let me call Remi and let her know what happened. She and Rascal are with the kids and she can be a little more vigilant without anyone else knowing. I agree we should get the other SUV and use it to watch but we're also finishing shopping because my kids are getting everything we planned."

"We've got your back."

"You got it, M-I-C."

She smiled at her sisters' comebacks and decided after she called Remington, she would put this out of her mind and enjoy shopping. They were all armed because they didn't go anywhere without being ready for the unexpected.

She wasn't looking forward to sharing the message with Bear and she had to choose her time because her grumpy guy might go on a rampage if his kids were threatened. Honestly she couldn't take the woman's words any other way than a threat. What the woman might not realize is Bear wasn't alone now and Winnie would burn the world before she allowed her man or children to be hurt.

Chapter Twenty-Four

Bear walked in and wrapped his arms around Winnie. She'd been staring out the back door for a while. Everyone had helped them put away most of the items the sisters had bought. Between the clothes, toys, books and kids' items they just *had to have* for his kids, he figured they were fine on clothes and toys for the next year. He had to admit the onesie for Joey with a motorcycle on it was cute. The things he was learning. Because of the mountain of clothes, each of the sisters had filled a basket of brand-new clothes and taken them home to wash.

He'd helped David with his bath tonight. Winnie had finally come in and told them they needed to get washed and quit playing with all the floating boats. He wanted to be a good dad. They would always miss their mom but he wanted to make their childhood a time that when they looked back on it, they couldn't remember anything but the love he and Winnie had for them. He would never allow them to go through what he'd experienced.

Everyone carried the baggage of their childhood and unfortunately, Bear was carrying a truckload of anger toward his incubator.

His kids wouldn't ever be touched by that evil because his sunbeam brightened every area of his life she touched. Their kids would be surrounded by the goodness she shared. He'd only been a dad for such a short time. Tucking David and Phoebe in tonight, kissing their foreheads and leaving the nightlight on for them felt like he'd been a part of their lives forever and he couldn't imagine his life without them in it.

Winnie sighed, then turned and hugged him. A shudder worked its way through her.

"Are you okay?"

She nodded, laying her hand against his cheek as she stared in his eyes.

"Remington and War are going to come over and stay with the kids a bit. I need to talk to you but I want to do it where we have some privacy."

A knock at the door had her leaving him wondering why they would need to have privacy. Remington and War walked in and sat at the island.

"Take as long as you need."

Winnie grasped his hand, leading him toward the door where she grabbed their jackets. He followed her, running through the scenarios of why they needed to be alone. Did she not want a family? Was she upset with him and the kids upsetting her house? Was something wrong with one of the kids? Had she learned something bad had happened to Phoebe or David while they were in emergency foster care? His thoughts tumbled as he followed Winnie to Remington's door.

She opened the door to Remington's house and took off her coat, turning to help him take his off. She clasped his cold hands and held them.

"Benton Carter. Stop. I can see every worst-case scenario running through your head. Pause. Wait until I tell you what's going on and then you can use your magnificent brain to help us figure out what our next move is, but we are in this together. I love you with my whole heart and we will face any challenge to our family together."

He took a deep breath, trying to follow Winnie's request. He listened to her recount their trip and concentrated on breathing in and out even though the thought of his incubator invading the very air Winnie breathed infuriated him. Winnie placed one hand against his chest and lightly ran her fingers of the other hand through his beard.

"Benton, listen to my voice. It's okay. We're in this together. Take another deep breath for me." He focused on Winnie's words and concentrated on her hands on him. Somehow his sunbeam knew what grounded him and pulled him out of his thoughts careening out of control.

"That's it, Benton. Focus on my voice and how much we love those kids already. I know you are the perfect dad for them because you'll help figure out how to keep them safe. Now can you look at something for me?"

He nodded, continuing to focus on his breathing. His sunbeam was gazing at him with her eyes filled with love. He could fall down the rabbit hole of what ifs or listen to his woman reminding him he wasn't alone and bask in her love. He'd never understood what people meant when they said they found their other half but Winnie had swept into his life. Nothing had been the same since and he'd be forever grateful.

"Sarah confirmed her name but I want your opinion. Is this her?"

He studied the picture. She'd colored her hair lighter again. He wasn't sure he even knew her real hair color. Her hair had ranged from blonde to black to red and everything in between. He assumed it was to stay one step ahead of the police. He focused on answering Winnie. It was the woman that birthed him but he was going to work to not allow her any power over him.

"Yes."

"Okay, now I have three options for tonight depending on where you're at. Option one, two of the prospects will go to the gym and Cannon will oversee you sparring with them if you need to work out some aggression. War said when you were upset at the precinct that helped. Option two, War will help you get falling down drunk so you can forget about all this either here at their house or at the clubhouse, or we have option three. You're infuriated at the woman who gave birth to you but you'll channel your aggression. I'll slide my hand inside your jeans, pull out your cock and all its fascinating decoration I adore, and worship it with my mouth until it's hard enough to pound granite. Then you'll bend me over the couch and have your way with me for as many times or as long as you need. Once we're exhausted we'll head home to bed to sleep. Rascal and my dad will come over to help us work through what scenarios she might have and figure out how we're going to keep her out of our lives permanently. Any option is fine, Benton, because I love all sides of my man but Remington and War don't know about option three so if that's your choice then we're on a time limit."

His sunbeam knew him better than he knew himself. If he'd been tackling this problem alone, option one would be the only way he'd get through it. Whether he sparred with someone or beat a heavy bag into submission, he'd have to expend his aggression.

He was going with option three. Naked, alone time with his woman had not happened since the kids came and he was hungry for her. To taste and touch her pale, smooth skin and to forget everything but being inside her tight sheath. With them regularly waking up in the night, he was making his choice.

He grasped Winnie's hair at her nape, leaned close and growled, "Option three," before he claimed her lips. Winnie kissed him back, then pulled back and nibbled his neck under his beard until her lips traveled to his shirt opening. She smiled and sank to her knees, unbuckling his belt and sliding down his zipper. Her words had inflamed him and tasting her already had him hard. He always loved her mouth on him but he didn't need her mouth to have him hard enough to pound granite as she said. Heck, half the time this week, he'd had to hide by their island because she'd brush against him when the kids were around and he'd hardened. His little minx had even smiled at him a couple times letting him know she'd known exactly what she was doing.

Her tongue licking against his cock head had him groaning. "Fuck!"

"Not yet, be patient." Her giggle as she laved his cock had him shuddering.

Patient. How the hell was he supposed to be patient when her tongue was laving underneath his head then licking down his shaft, twirling against his piercing? His toes curled and his spine tingled so he grasped her face, pulling her off him.

"Baby, I can't let you or I'll blow down your throat. Lose the jeans and boots then bare that gorgeous ass to me."

His woman wasted no time, removing her clothes then holding up one finger and running down the hall. She ran back in with a sheet, laying it over the back of the couch with some trailing onto the floor.

"I can't help the house will smell like sex but I can honestly tell Remington we didn't have sex against any piece of furniture in her house."

He chuckled, running his hand up and down his shaft while he watched Winnie get situated. She looked over her shoulder with her eyebrow cocked. The man who rarely smiled's face hurt a little from how happy his woman made him. He trailed a finger down her spine, grinning at her trembling.

"What are you waiting for?"

He laid one hand against her back, sliding his other between her legs. He circled her nub, feeling a shudder work through her as he spread the wetness all around it and slowly sank a finger inside her wet heat.

"Feels like someone wants this as much as I do." He leaned over, laving kisses against his woman's cheeks then nipping at her ass.

"Benton, get your cock inside me now." His woman deserved everything she wanted and honestly, he wasn't sure he could make this last. Her skin in the light of the lamp had him wanting to explore every inch of her, especially her tattoo on her shoulder. He loved the wings spread with the shading.

"Gladly, Sunbeam. I'd hate for this pretty pussy to be neglected."

Bear notched himself at her core then thrust inside in one stroke, relishing the feeling as he filled his woman. This would be their quickest time yet. He was hungry for her and her words and mouth had fired him up. Her sheath was better than anything he'd imagined.

"Harder and faster. I'm so close." She groaned, pushing back against him.

He pulled out, gliding back in, her pussy clasping him tight and rippling around him. So close. Thank fuck she was on the edge. He pounded harder into her as he slid his finger around and rubbed Winnie, setting off fireworks for them both.

He tried to catch his breath and wasn't ashamed at the tears that came to his eyes. He was home. The place he'd always dreamed of but never thought he'd have. His sunbeam would be beside him. He pulled her up off the couch, leaning her back against his chest. He turned her head to brush a kiss against her lips.

"I love you. We'll get through this together because you're the light that leads me home, Sunbeam."

Chapter Twenty-Five

Winnie relished Bear's arm around her. He grounded her when she wanted to hunt down Bear's bio-mom and rip her limb from limb. Bear had needed to hold on to her as much as she needed his touch. He'd spent the last twenty minutes going through all the times she'd blown up his life.

Rascal's face had gotten progressively redder until she worried he'd explode. She wasn't sure if he was upset at Bear or Bio-mom but he would not be chastising Bear. She firmly believed if Bear would have gotten help over the years he might have shared what was happening to him. She wouldn't fault Rascal because he'd grown up in the age where people weren't as open about mental health. Opinions regarding seeking help had changed over the years.

Rascal stood up as Bear finished. Striding around the table, he pulled Bear out of his seat, wrapping his arm around him and holding his head clasped in his large hand.

"I'm so sorry I didn't protect you from her. Son, you're not alone. We'll figure this out and get her out of your life forever."

Bear had let go of her hand when his dad grabbed him but her dad had wrapped his arm around her. She laid her head on his shoulder.

"You've got a good one there, Winchester. I couldn't have asked for a better man for you. We've got your back."

This was what she wanted to give her kids. The family who wrapped you in their loving arms when things were at their worst. The ones who picked you up when you were too tired to go it on your own.

Everyone settled down and sat back down. She knew it was a struggle for Rascal, Baron, and Locks to let the younger generation lead. She admired them for passing the torch but family dynamics were hard.

"Sarah and Scoop have worked and identified two possible places where…"

"Gnat is staying," Beth interrupted War.

"Gnat?" War questioned.

"Well, Bear's called her incubator which is accurate but a mouthful. Winnie calls her Bio-mom which I think is being generous because she doesn't deserve the title mom. Sorry, Bear, if that offends you. I had a lot of other things to call her but that would have required multiple donations to the swear jar, so I like Gnat. Gnats are annoying but inconsequential in the scheme of life. When we get through showing her to never mess with the Franks daughters or the Bluff Creek Brotherhood MC, she will be a smashed gnat—inconsequential in any of our lives."

"Okay, so they've identified two possible places where Gnat is staying. We have two people Locks and Remington thought would be good from the Topeka office to do reconnaissance. Gnat most likely saw Beth and we don't want her knowing we're on to them. In the short term, until we can get a better barrier, Locks will park a feed truck in front of the gate to the houses. Jesse is working on a secondary way in and we'll just have to have one of us move it when we go in and out. I think anything is worth keeping the kids safe."

"Amen, brother," echoed from multiple brothers.

"Now, I believe Bear has something he'd like to say."

Bear stood up beside her and turned her chair toward him. "Sunbeam, it seems by MC standards I've done everything out of order, but our story has unfolded exactly as it was supposed to. When I didn't think I was good enough for you, you knocked and beat on my hardened heart until I opened up to let the sun in. I never imagined in my forties I'd be blessed with a woman who knows me better than I know myself and take on three children as if it had been planned all along. Things are crazy right now but you've taught me we're all better together. You already said yes to marrying me but will you ride with me until I leave this earth?"

Scoop handed Bear the cut he'd been hiding underneath the table.

She stood, letting Bear put it on her. Turning to him, she kissed his lips. "I will. Until our time on earth ends."

She loved her cut but she loved even more what had been put on Bear's cut. She didn't know how she'd missed it when they sat down but she remembered he'd had a sweatshirt on his lap. He'd added a patch that read *Property of Bear's Sunbeam.*

"Great. Now let's go have some of the food I can smell Mom cooking up and fuel up. We've got this."

Chapter Twenty-Six

Bear helped David out of the car seat and situated his hat back on his head. David had let him know quite loudly he didn't like his hat. Of course, he was going to blame Grant. Grant had said hats were stupid and Roam had corrected him.

Winnie had wanted them to spend time with the kids individually and he'd agreed it was needed. Phoebe talked a lot but David was quiet. He and Winnie both wanted to make sure each child had their own individual time.

Winnie and a couple of her sisters were visiting a farm to pick up a dog for Beth. The farm also had kittens and lambs that Winnie said Phoebe could pet.

Roam had suggested they take the boys to see a colt that had just been born. One of the guys Roam had done a tattoo for had given Roam an open invitation to bring his kids out. So he and Roam had loaded up Grant and David to leave when Rascal, Baron, and Locks had decided to invade their outing. Luckily their SUV seated seven.

"Roam, glad you could make it. Are you guys ready to see the colt?"

The boys nodded. David was still leery around people he didn't know and tugged on Bear's jeans to lift him up. Bear sat him on his hip then leaned close to his ear.

"Let's go see the baby horse. I haven't ever seen one this young so I'll need you to hug me tight."

David nodded and wrapped his little arm around Bear's neck, tucking his head against Bear's chest. Bear swallowed and vowed he wasn't going to get misty-eyed at his son leaning on him, trusting Bear to keep him safe.

David closed his nose with his fingers when the smell of horses and manure reached their noses.

Grant turned around to where he'd run and looked for David. "Smells like poop but not as bad as sissy's."

Baron chuckled, patting Grant's head. "Let's not tell that to your sister, okay?"

Grant rolled his eyes. "Too many don'ts. Don't yell when sissy's sleeping. Don't help Casper play in the hose."

"Life's really rough, isn't it, Grant? Do you want to see the colt or do you want to go whine in the car?" Roam stared at Grant, waiting for his answer. He couldn't wait until David felt comfortable enough to whine about something.

"Colt, please."

They paused at the door to the stall. The colt was eating. Grant crawled up the stall door and balanced on the bottom step. Bear stepped closer so David could watch.

"Is he drinkin' from her boobies? Mom fed sissy and bubba like that til she left."

Bear was thankful for the rancher who answered Grant's question. His mother was a sore subject for Roam.

"Yes. His mom will do that until he can eat on his own. The colt is new enough we can't have everyone pet her yet but I have something else you can pet. Follow me."

He opened the last stall, inviting them all in. A mother dog and what looked like eight puppies ran around the stall. David strained to get down and Bear let him go. David promptly sat down when two puppies licked his face. He giggled and Bear decided it was a sound he wanted to hear the rest of his life.

David had laughed a couple times but this was a deep belly laugh. He was hugging the puppies, smiling and laughing as they licked his hands. Grant was right there beside him holding a puppy while another tried to chew on his cap he'd dropped.

"What are they?" Rascal questioned.

"By looking at them, I think a mix of Golden Retriever and Australian Shepherd. The mom showed up here a month ago, pregnant, skinny and covered in fleas. People dump unwanted animals near the farm entrance all the time. You know how it is."

They all nodded. Someone got an animal then decided it wasn't worth the time and dumped it in a driveway and left. The shop had a couple cats they were feeding now and taking care of because they'd been dropped at the gate.

Bear had a soft heart for animals. He still remembered when he'd come to the MC that Roam and War had their very own dogs. He'd wanted one so bad but had been too scared to ask his dad for one. His mom had taught him a painful lesson about asking for things but Rascal had known what he wanted. One morning Rascal had left him with Regina and Kathryn. When he returned, he'd brought an eight-month-old puppy. That dog had gotten him through some tough times. His dad had even let the dog sleep in his room, more often than not he'd been in his bed.

"How old are the puppies and what are you doing with them?" If they were old enough, his son was going home with a puppy today.

"They're twelve weeks old and I need to find homes for them."

Grant looked at Roam but David didn't even look at him. His son needed to learn how to dream and wish and want for things he hadn't before. He was sure Winnie would be okay with him getting the kids a puppy. She loved animals and loved their children, too.

"David, what do you think about picking out a puppy to have at our house? I bet you and Phoebe can help us take care of one."

His son raised his head with the biggest smile he'd ever seen on his face. "Really?"

The incredulity in his son's voice had him leaning down and nodding. "Pick out the one you want."

David scrambled to start playing with and holding different puppies. Grant's face was looking at his dad.

"I'm okay with you getting one, too, if Papa thinks Nana will be okay with a puppy. We're living with them now."

"Son, haven't I taught you anything? Sometimes it's better to ask forgiveness than permission. How do you think you and your brother got puppies that first year?"

Roam leaned down, chucked Grant under the chin and motioned to the puppies. "Pick out your new dog, son."

Grant jumped up and did a shimmy and a shake. "C'mon, David. We're getting puppies."

Roam looked over at his client. "I can't decide whether to discount your next tattoo or charge you double at the bait and switch. Come see my new horse then bam, go home with a new puppy."

"Whatever you want to do, man."

"This one, Dad. I'm going to call him Dog." Grant held up a cute fluffy puppy, with white, cream and brown mottled fur.

"Son, you can't call him Dog. He needs a real name." Grant's smile fell and he sniffed, turning away from his dad.

"Grant, why don't you and Papa talk on the way back and think up names."

David picked up a fluffy puppy with white and gray fur. "This one but gots to ask Phoebe to help."

Bear picked up David and the dog, snuggling them close. "You got it, buddy."

Winnie listened to her sisters answer all Phoebe's questions about where they were going and what would they see. It was Beth's idea for an excursion and she had wanted to keep it a secret.

"Phoebe, I told you. You'll find out when we get there. That's what a surprise is."

Phoebe's sigh echoed through the SUV. Sarah, Jesse, and Remington all hid their smiles. Winnie was positive they were waiting to see what she'd do. Well, she was doing nothing. In fact, she thought Phoebe was hysterical with letting Beth know she didn't appreciate having to wait.

Beth made the turn on the farm road and Winnie shifted in her seat. She was almost as excited as Beth. Beth was picking up three dogs from the training center one of the neighborhood farms ran. Neighborhood was relative living out in western Kansas. They'd driven forty-five minutes to get to the farm.

Since Beth was on surveillance so much by herself, she'd decided to get a companion. At least it had started as one companion but after much consideration, Beth was getting three dogs. Winnie couldn't wait to see what she'd picked but Beth had even kept the secret from her sisters about which dogs she'd decided on.

"Okay, Phoebe, here's the deal. I'm picking up three dogs to help me in my job but I have to be gone sometimes and I can't take all three. Do you think you'd like to help Jesse take care of my dogs when I'm gone and play with them? When I'm home I'll probably need some help, too."

"Yeah!" Phoebe screamed, having Winnie wishing Beth would have waited until they were outside the vehicle.

They all exited the car with Phoebe climbing over Sarah in her haste to get to the dogs.

"Beth, they're waiting for you."

"Thanks."

He led them into the building and three dogs were lying on mats in the front room. Winnie appreciated how clean the facility smelled. The dogs were alert and watching them.

"Why don't you call them individually and test how they do."

Beth grinned. "Lilly, come."

A darling black Cocker Spaniel ran over to Beth and rubbed up against her. She had a cute little vest or whatever the trainers called it with lettering that said service animal. Beth petted her head, rubbing underneath her chin where she had a splotch of white. Lilly looked about twenty pounds and the perfect size to cuddle with on a couch. Beth snapped the leash on Lilly's vest and handed it to Remington, then walked across the room and stood.

"Moss, headquarters."

At Beth's words, the mottled gray and white Schnauzer ran across the room then stopped and sat, waiting at attention. Beth leaned down, rubbing his head. "What a good, good boy."

Beth clipped a leash on his collar and brought him over to Sarah. She then walked over where a small piece of carpeting was. She stood then slowly dropped to her knees, imitating a fall. "Dolly, protect."

Dolly ran over to Beth, turning with her back to her and growling at them. Beth leaned up, saying, "Cease." The dog turned toward her and sat with her face on her leg. "Good girl. You're such a good girl."

She stood up, clipped a leash on the collar and led her over to Winnie. "Well, Phoebe, you think you can help me?"

"Yes. I'll be the bestest helper."

The adults giggled as Phoebe wrapped her arms around Lilly, squeezing her a little.

"Well, Phoebe, Beth told me you might want to check out some of my other animals, too. Would you like to see my chickens?"

Winnie loved watching the expressions cross Phoebe's face. He opened the door to another area which had large penned areas with doors to the outside in each area. Most areas were empty. Two had animals in them. The first had what Winnie thought were either miniature horses or miniature donkeys. She had to admit, she might live in the country but had zero interest in large four-legged creatures.

"What are those?" Phoebe paused and pointed. "Can I pet 'em?"

"They are miniature ponies. I'm boarding them for a neighbor who goes to Texas during the winter months. And yes, you may pet them. Good job asking first." He pulled a couple sugar cubes out of a bag hanging on the door. "Here, you can give them one of these, too. Lay your hand flat and they'll use their tongue to get it."

Phoebe flattened her hand and held it out to the closest pony once he laid the sugar cube there. The pony leaned out and licked the cube off.

Phoebe giggled and scrunched up her nose. "That tickled."

After feeding the one, she had to make sure the other didn't feel neglected. Then he led them down the aisles like the pied piper with all of them following. Phoebe pointed to the last area before they went outside.

"Why is that one by itself?"

Winnie glanced where Phoebe was pointing to see a black fluffy puppy with a white area on its tummy.

"She's part of a litter I trained. She'll mind but she'd rather play than work."

"What's going to happen to her? She looks lonely." Phoebe's hand curled around the wire of the pen door.

"I'll find her a good home where she can play and not have to be a working dog like the dogs Beth is taking home."

Phoebe seemed satisfied with his answer and followed him out to see the chickens in the pen. Winnie paused, looking at the dog all alone in the pen. She remembered the dogs they'd had over the years. She and her sisters had learned a great deal about discipline and life taking care of them. She also remembered pouring her heart out to their dog Ashley when her sisters had hurt her feelings.

The dog stood up and walked over to the edge of the pen and whined at her. She leaned down, sliding her fingers in to let the puppy lick. She may be a sucker because she wasn't going to think about adding another thing to take care of when she and Bear had only had the kids a short time. She wasn't going to think about how Joey was less than three weeks old. She was going to imagine the laughter and hugs as the kids played with the dog. They returned before she finished weighing the pros and cons of getting another thing to take care of. Her sisters and Phoebe headed back to the main office.

When the trainer closed the door behind him and walked over to the pen, Winnie couldn't resist asking him, "How much?"

He smiled and patted her arm. "Consider him a bonus for the help you all gave my bottom line with the purchase of training for the three dogs. Do you want to take him today?"

She nodded. Glancing behind her, she saw the door to the front room closing, leaving her and the owner alone. "Yes, could you grab a leash? I want to head out there and then would you deliver him to my daughter, Phoebe?"

"Yes. I'd be happy to. She's going to be a very happy little girl."

Winnie felt like skipping down the hallway to the front area. She was probably freaking crazy but how hard could it be to add one little dog to their family?

She came through the door and saw Phoebe petting Lilly, then Dolly, then Moss, and starting all over again. Sarah smiled. "She wants to make sure they don't get jealous of each other."

Winnie's sisters stared at her expectantly. Remi's eyebrow was cocked up because Remi knew her better than anyone.

She'd probably already figured out Winnie had gotten Phoebe a dog.

The owner walked through with the puppy on a leash. He headed over to Phoebe.

"Phoebe, your mom told me to deliver him to you."

Phoebe's eyes were round and wide. She turned to look at Winnie. Winnie nodded and smiled.

"Thank you!" Phoebe screamed and grabbed the puppy around his body. She sat down and buried her face in his neck. "I will always love you, I promise. We'll be bestest friends forever."

Chapter Twenty-Seven

Bear sat on the floor rolling the ball to David and watching the puppy grab it in its mouth. Once they'd gotten back to the house, Baron had offered to go buy supplies for the puppy. He was probably avoiding being in their house when Regina discovered Roam had brought home a puppy. Bear had no doubt Regina would fall in love with it just like Roam and Grant did.

David looked like he was fading fast after their busy morning. Maybe he and the puppy could lie down and watch a show. Rascal was in the kitchen making sandwiches for lunch and had already indicated he had an idea for fencing in an area to let the puppy out in. Bear was on board with that. He didn't want to have to go out on cold mornings with the dog but they had coyotes around and other critters that might hurt the puppy.

Rascal had been a big help but he'd mentioned he didn't want to overstay his welcome at Locks' house. Bear wasn't quite ready to have Rascal live in the house with them because his dad needed his alone time. Maybe he could offer the RV he'd bought to his dad temporarily. They could park it in between the house and the garage. His dad would have his own space but be close enough he could visit whenever he wanted.

Although he had no problem making the puppy decision on his own, he'd wait and discuss moving his dad next door to them with Winnie. He couldn't wait to see Phoebe's face when David showed her the puppy. A puppy couldn't bring back their mom but every little thing showing them this was home would help them feel comfortable.

The slam of car doors had his heart speeding up. Now he was starting to imagine all the bad ways Winnie could react to him getting a dog without asking her. She might decide he and the kids weren't worth the trouble.

The door slammed as Phoebe stumbled into the room screaming, "Look what we got!"

Winnie helped her not fall then smiled tentatively, then he noticed the puppy his daughter was carrying. He snickered, then couldn't help laughing. He pointed toward David in the recliner. He laughed harder at Winnie's eyes widening.

"We gots two?!" David yelled.

Rascal walked in from the kitchen then joined in the laughter as he took in the situation.

"Honey, I guess it's okay we got a puppy," Winnie joked as she smiled then kissed his mouth. "I'd hoped you wouldn't be mad I got a puppy without asking but, umm, I somehow think you're okay with it."

Winnie's sisters immediately checked out David's dog. Bear rubbed his chest and hugged Winnie a little tighter at the ache of watching David beam as the girls ooh'd and ahh'd over his puppy. He'd had so many doubts but each day with Winnie and their families showed him happiness was possible.

His sunbeam had shown him love could conquer all.

Chapter Twenty-Eight

Winnie glanced at the text Sarah had sent.

Sarah: Think I've located Gnat. Haven't shared with Scoop. Thoughts?

Beth: I think we visit Gnat and put the fear of the Franks sisters in her. Two options—leave Bear alone or suffer our wrath.

Jesse: Agreed.

Remington: I'm up for whatever Winnie wants. If we don't want the guys to know, though, we'll need a good excuse.

What she wanted was to keep her family safe and never have Bear have to deal with Gnat again. She didn't want to necessarily lie to Bear but she didn't want talking about Gnat to bring him down again.

The last two weeks with the kids had been wonderful. They'd gotten into a routine. Rascal had moved into the RV next to their house. They'd hooked it up to water and electricity. They'd even modified some things to guarantee the pipes didn't freeze.

They'd also added a small, fenced area where the dogs could go out and do their business without someone having to be with them the whole time. Rascal had taken to watching Joey and the dogs if he didn't have any client appointments. If he did, Lock came and subbed in.

She and Bear had sat them down last week and had a talk about presents. The kids had plenty and they loved both Papas equally. They'd all four agreed on a moratorium on presents until birthdays or holidays. She and Bear were fine with all the things they'd all showered on the kids but she didn't want it to be a habit. She and her sisters had learned to work for stuff when they were older and she wanted the kids to have the same. Plus she didn't want to have to add on to the house or build another because of the gifts the Papas were buying.

Her stomach ached at Gnat getting close to Bear or the kids. She didn't like misleading Bear but if he knew, he'd want to go along. His protective instinct for her and the kids was through the roof. This was one time Winnie was going to protect Bear.

Winnie: I hate the thought of lying to Bear but we need to scare her enough that she leaves us alone.

Beth: What if scaring her doesn't work? Do you have the next step?

Winnie: Thinking it through. I'm open to suggestions.

Remington: Okay. So we're planning a girls' trip to Kansas City next weekend. We'll tell the guys we're taking two SUVs so we can bring back plenty of items. Sarah, we need a place to stay, not a hotel. Jesse, I want the SUVs loaded for any eventuality. I think we need to invite Regina.

Winnie: Why?

Remington: She's badass and also knows Gnat. We need intel plus taking Regina will put the guys in charge of all the kids. They'll be too busy taking care of kids to think of what we're doing.

Jesse: And that's why you're in charge. You're devious, big sis. Got it.

Sarah: We're not going to do anything we need alibis for, will we? If so, I need to work on that before we go.

Winnie: This is a TALK!! No we don't need alibis.

Although Winnie would love to make sure Gnat never bothered Bear again, she'd never decided to kill anyone. She'd shot and killed an assailant when she was on a security job. He'd been after her client and she'd defended them both.

Thinking about her kids and Bear, though, made her wonder how far she would go to keep them safe. If someone came at her kids, she'd defend them with everything she had. She'd fallen in love with each of them. Phoebe, David and even little Joey had wormed their way into her heart until she couldn't imagine a life without them.

The social worker had visited and approved everything for the moment. Winnie wanted to make everything official but her and Bear being married would make it easier and anything with bureaucrats involved made things harder. Their social worker said she'd be back in a month but in the meantime, Bear had access to everything at the kids' house. The MC was sending a couple members to pack up the house. Beth had indicated most of it was shredded but with Gnat in the picture, they wanted every scrap from the house. The crime scene had been released. Bear planned on checking with the department to see if there were any leads.

Remington: Are we in agreement?

Winnie: Yes. We are going to have a chat with Gnat and explain the consequences of continuing to harass Bear.

Beth: I'm all for that but I think Sarah should continue digging into Gnat. There's no way she's survived all these years without stepping over a couple lines.

Sarah: Yep. Mint Chocolate Chip is digging into money and how she's survived. Sure, Bear's given her a lot of cash over the years but not enough to survive as long as she has.

Winnie: Scoop doesn't know you found her, right?
Sarah: Nope. We're good. I'm following her and her connections. He's following the money.

Winnie turned back to her schedule for the gym. They were getting busy enough and with the addition of the kids, she didn't want to increase her hours. She'd pulled as many people to help as she could from the MC and her sisters. She'd need to look at hiring someone to help. She added modifying a kids' room to her list for the gym. Sometimes she wanted to be able to bring the kids with her but there wasn't a good place they could hang out.

Her whole attitude had changed with the kids filling up her life. She hated missing any second and couldn't imagine it would get any easier, especially as Joey started doing all his firsts, like rolling over and crawling.

Despite growing up with the MC and the skirmishes that had happened over the years, she'd always known her parents would keep her safe. Once her dad deemed them old enough, he worked with them on how to stay safe. She wanted that for her kids, which meant it was time to scare Gnat and have her fly far, far away.

Winnie: Who is contacting Regina? Then we can tell the guys.

Remington: I'm seeing her today. I will. We're here for you, Winnie.

Beth: We might need another code for a clandestine op without the guys.

Jesse: I like it.

Sarah: Got your back, Winnie. Everybody has their assignments and I'm not adding any more codes. Remi's hunk just had me print cards up with the codes for the guys because he couldn't remember them all. Remi must have blown his mind with sex because how hard is it to remember nine codes?

Remington: Hey, I'm good. What can I say? My man is a delicious treat I enjoy sampling regularly, but I agree. We might need more codes.

Jesse: Now you're just being mean for those of us not getting any, right, Sarah?

Beth: WTF? Who do you think I'm supposedly doing? It's been a long dry spell for me too.

Jesse: Sorry.

Sarah: I have a client that just walked in. I'm out.

Chapter Twenty-Nine

Winnie drummed her fingers on the dashboard, waiting for the signal. They'd dropped some of their stuff off at the house they were staying at and then waited until dark to head to Gnat's.

Sarah reached over and placed her hand on Winnie's. "It will be okay. We'll take care of this nuisance and then you can go back to the amazing life you're starting with your man."

"I know. I just want this over. How long can it take Beth and Remington to check out the place?"

"Time passes slowly when you're waiting on people. They've been gone five minutes. We allotted eight to ten. Give your sisters time to confirm who's in the house."

Regina's calm voice washed over Winnie, relaxing her a little. Regina and Winnie's mom had both had that calming influence with their family and children. Winnie wished she would have learned that or absorbed it from being around them but it was her personality. Winnie was the person who could see the light on the darkest day but she was also the one who might fly off the handle if she was angry.

Winnie jerked at the tap on her window. She rolled it down, waiting for the go ahead.

"She's alone in the front room. Two from the front, two from the back and two from the garage. Let's do this." Remington's no-nonsense approach had Winnie double-checking her weapon.

When she had time later, she'd remember Sarah's surprise at the multiple guns and knives Regina had brought. What did she think a woman who had stood by her man for over forty years in an MC would bring to have a chat with someone threatening them?

"Countdown in three, two, one. Breach."

Remington's peaceful voice through her ear mic was a contrast to the sound as they entered Gnat's residence.

Winnie scanned the kitchen and entered the hall. "Kitchen clear."

Beth's voice echoed from the front room. "I wouldn't do that if I were you. Sit your ass back down and stay there. We're just here for a chat."

"A chat with guns?" Gnat screeched.

"Well, we'll start with a chat but if you don't cooperate, I have no problem using other persuasive tools."

Winnie shivered at the coldness in Regina's tone. The sweet, loving grandmother had morphed into someone Winnie didn't want to meet in a dark alley.

"I might have known you'd be here with them, bitch," Gnat whined.

Regina nodded at Remington and Winnie. Winnie wanted the lead. She craved to see fear on Gnat's face. The same type of fear her man had experienced his whole life whenever he was subjected to Gnat exploding into his life.

Winnie walked over in front of Gnat, who was sitting on the couch with her hands on her lap.

"We're here for a chat. Bear is mine and with me, comes my whole fucking family. You will never and I mean never go near him again or anyone in my family. Just because I think you might be a little dense, I'm going to be clear. Bluff Creek is off limits to you, meaning you don't even use the highway that passes by it to get somewhere. If you happen to see Bear or anyone in my family someplace where you're at, fucking run until you're at least ten miles away."

Gnat laughed, which wasn't what Winnie was expecting. If six armed women had broken into her house, she'd be worried.

"It's funny you think you have control. Enjoy those babies while you can. You won't have them long."

Winnie held her gun up toward Gnat's face and leaned over her. Gnat threatening her children had anger overtaking her. "Explain."

"Oh, I'm not going to explain. You'll find out soon enough then everything in his world will fall apart. Get out of my house before I call the cops."

Winnie had no idea what was going on but this wasn't how she'd envisioned Bear's incubator. Winnie nodded her head at Sarah and Beth to search the house. They'd worked together long enough they didn't need words. Regina touched shoulders with Winnie, tilting her head toward Gnat questioningly.

Winnie nodded. If Regina could get through to her better, then more power to her. Nothing was making sense. She glanced around the house. It was a nice three-bedroom ranch style. The couch and recliners along with the television looked new and definitely hadn't been from a thrift store. If Gnat was so hard up for money she was squeezing Bear for it, then how was she affording this house?

"Kendra, what's going on?" Regina sat down on the couch beside Gnat. If Winnie hadn't heard Regina talking in the car, she'd assume Regina was sitting down with her best friend.

"Oh look, Baron's little goody two shoes bride wants to help me. I don't need your help. I've got friends now."

Regina stared at Gnat for a minute. Winnie couldn't tell if Regina was trying to unnerve Gnat or was thinking through what to do next. Regina smiled and then slid closer to Gnat. She leaned close, whispering in her ear. Gnat's confident smile dimmed as Regina continued talking.

Sarah and Beth returned. Sarah nodded. Maybe whatever Sarah and Beth had found would help.

Regina stood up. "Any last words you need to tell her, Winnie?"

"I'll reiterate this to you just in case you missed it. Do not contact Bear. Do not do anything in regards to the children and keep at least ten miles between you and Bear. If you choose to violate any of the rules, I'll assume you want the consequences."

"Fuck you and your consequences. When this is all over, you'll be gone and I'll be left standing to spit over your graves."

Remington walked closer, nudging Winnie to the side. "Now see, we were just here to deliver a message but you had to escalate it. I can't decide if you're just stupid or trying to provoke something." Remington cocked her eyebrow at Sarah.

"Nothing's recording. I'm jamming anything but I didn't detect any devices."

"Remington, if we're going to need to dispose of something, I'm going to need to get the trash bags from the car. You didn't mention we'd be going scorched earth when we walked up."

Remington rolled her eyes then stared at Gnat. "As the oldest, I kind of have a bit of a temper. We have to plan for all eventualities hence the dark clothes. Blood is such a pain to get out of white clothes. I guess it all comes down to you. Are you going to continue to threaten us or are you going to agree to abide by the rules?"

Remington walked closer, grabbed Gnat's hair, and tilted her head back. Sliding her gun up against her chin, she leaned down to whisper, "I'm good with either but it's your call."

Gnat jerked her head back from the gun, rolling her eyes to scrutinize each of them. Winnie wondered what she'd choose. Killing Gnat would be crossing a line for them and despite wanting to protect Bear, she wasn't there yet.

"I'll follow your stupid rules."

Remington released Gnat, giving her a little shove as she backed away. "Ladies, are we done here?"

Everyone nodded but Regina. "How about you ladies go out the front door? I have one more thing to say to Kendra before we leave."

Winnie decided as long as there wasn't any possibility of Regina getting hurt, she didn't see any harm in it. They walked on the front porch and waited for Regina. A couple minutes later, Regina walked out. Winnie had tried to listen but couldn't hear anything from inside the house. Once they were buckled in, Winnie couldn't wait any longer.

"What did you say to her?"

Regina smirked. "I gave her a little reminder."

"What type of reminder?" Sarah asked.

"The kind where I emphasized where you all might be bound by the guidelines for bail bonds and bounty hunting, I'm not. I told her I'd been in an MC for over forty years and I wasn't going to allow her to hurt my family."

Beth backed up the SUV and drove around the block, then parked in a nearby driveway. Beth pulled a phone out of the glovebox and dialed. She laid it on the console, putting it on speaker.

"911, what's your emergency?"

"Well, I'm not sure. There's this house that people are going in and out of. Like lots of traffic. Then I saw the lady walk out of the house and take a package to a car waiting on the street. He handed her money then left."

"Ma'am, what address is this happening at?"

"1911 Sycamore Street."

"Ma'am, I need you to wait around for the police."

"Oh no, I can't do that. My mom will kill me if she finds out I snuck out of the house."

"Honey, your mom..."

"No, I...I can't."

Beth had added a little hiccup and cry at the end of her words before she hung up, turned the phone off and pulled the sim card out.

"What the hell, Beth? What happens when they get there and realize it's a prank call?"

Beth turned around and looked at her sisters. "I get you all don't get to see me in the field often but I've seen a lot on surveillance and if I say so myself, I'm phenomenal at my job. I put a scale, baggies and five hundred grams of weed in her kitchen in plain sight from the back door. We need to know who the people in high places are. She'll either be taken in tonight by police officers or someone else is going to keep her out of jail."

Winnie stared at her sister. "You're freaking brilliant. Wait...did we have weed in the car all the way up here?"

Beth rolled her eyes. "Of course not. Someone in town owed me a favor and was more than happy to borrow some for me."

"Borrow some?"

Winnie turned to Remi, shushing her and pointing. A dark brown sedan pulled up to the curb within five minutes. Winnie grabbed some binoculars so she could see who got out better. A man in a suit exited the car and walked up to the house. Average height with graying hair. He was a little thicker with a paunch hanging over his belt, pushing his jacket open. Winnie thought he looked familiar but she wasn't sure where she recognized him from.

Beth had taken her camera and was snapping pictures of the car and the man getting out and walking to the door.

Winnie wasn't sure what was going on but she knew there was more to Gnat than she'd thought. Remington had a pair of binoculars trained on the front door and was watching. He'd been in the house about five minutes before he exited. Remington gasped as he walked toward his vehicle. Beth continued taking pictures.

"Guys, this just got a little more complicated," Remington said.

"Why?" Winnie asked. What could be more complicated?

"Sarah, do you recognize him? I'm right, aren't I?"

"Yep. Remington had me do deep dives on the guys before they did security with us. I'll want to confirm when I get my computer on at the room but I'm almost positive that's Bear and War's ex-chief of police."

"Friggin' hell. The same chief of police all the guys were positive was dirty but they couldn't prove? Now we're going to have to let the guys know what we did," Remington growled.

Friggin' hell was right. Bear wasn't going to be happy but also, what were they going to do? How did Gnat and the guys' ex-chief get tied up together and how long had it been going on?

"I'm not looking forward to sharing it so I say we have a good night's sleep then do some power shopping. I have a feeling no one is going to be happy with us after we come clean."

Chapter Thirty

Winnie situated Joey in her arms and nudged his mouth with the nipple—not that her little man needed any help. He'd turned into quite the eater. She was so happy with the kids but she wasn't looking forward to sharing with Bear about what they'd found out.

They'd shopped and then headed home. Having everything hanging over their heads had put a damper on their fun. More than half the drive was spent discussing the best way to notify the guys. She didn't even appreciate the rolling hills between Medicine Lodge and Coldwater because she was petrified knowing about Gnat and his chief would set Bear back.

Bear had met weekly with the counselor they'd found. Bear's was a different one than Winnie had gone to. Hers had specialized in grief but he'd recommended one of the members of his practice whose specialty was PTSD and anxiety over trauma. The first couple of times, she hadn't thought it was helping because Bear's nightmares had increased but then once he'd opened up more, she'd seen a difference.

With it being Sunday night, he'd only have a day until his appointment, though he had an emergency number he could call if he needed.

Bear walked in, leaned down, and kissed Joey's forehead. His lips were close to hers as he stood up and he leaned in to brush a kiss across her lips, too. "Where's the rest of our kiddos?"

"Beth and Jesse took them and the puppies all over to play in the garage. Jesse mentioned something about an obstacle course. I'm not really sure if it was for the puppies or the kids."

He opened the refrigerator and grabbed a beer. "Do you want one?"

She shook her head. If she drank anything, she'd probably have it all come up again. She was nervous and a tad nauseous thinking about telling Bear.

The doorbell ringing had her pausing. A reprieve would be nice but she had to tell him.

"Guess we have company." Bear led Rascal and Locks back into the room.

"What are you guys doing here? Just over to see the kids?" She tried to inject a hopeful note in her voice but her heart was pounding and it was so hot in the room.

Rascal grabbed an extra chair from the table and pulled it over in front of her. He motioned Bear to sit down. Locks grabbed a chair, joining the group.

"Well, spit it out, Winnie. Regina told us to come over and you'd explain about some adventure you and your sisters got into."

Holding Joey was helping but she still felt off. Bear leaned over and put his hand on her thigh. "Sunbeam, you're worrying me with your breathing. Whatever it is, we can get through it together." He rubbed her thigh and she focused on breathing. She'd been worried about Bear and she still was, but she'd forgotten that with their family, she'd never be alone.

"I didn't want to tell you because I'm worried dealing with it will bring up all the horrible things you've dealt with, but you need to know."

Bear listened to Winnie recount what they'd really done when they were supposedly out shopping. He was fucking impressed with their plans and who knew the youngest sister would have the biggest balls of all of them?

He glanced over at his dad and Locks. Both were tense, ready to take him to the ground if he tried to head off half-cocked without a plan. What they didn't realize was his sunbeam had finally gotten through the last quarter inch and pounded it into his brain that his analytical thinking was a blessing to his family. He was going to use everything at his disposal to figure out how and why their old chief was working with his mom and what their plan was.

He wanted to paddle Winnie's ass and make sure she never put herself in danger again but that wasn't who she was. She was a fierce, badass woman who would protect her family to her last breath. He was going to nurture that amazing quality, not stifle it.

Between Scoop and Sarah, they could find out why those two were spending time together and why Gnat was so confident they wouldn't have the kids for long. Did Gnat or the chief have something to do with Cassidy's death?

"Bear, are you okay?" Rascal questioned.

"I'm not okay in the fact that those two seem to be gunning for my kids but we're going to gather information, figure out what their end game is, and thwart everything because these kids deserve the world. Sunbeam and I are going to give that to them. I don't care if the MC has to call up the Texas chapter and any of our other allies but it will be a fucking frozen day in hell before she breathes the same air as my kids."

Locks chuckled. "I don't think we need to worry about Bear, Rascal. I think he's the clearest he's ever been. Remington told me a message to give you which I now understand. She has four teams rotating on eight-hour shifts. Two teams on each individual gathering info."

He got out of the chair, kneeling on the floor by Winnie. Sliding his hand into her hair, he claimed her lips. He needed to taste his sunbeam and remember what they were fighting for.

"I should have known the perfect woman for me wouldn't need rescued. She'd stand toe to toe against our foe and side by side with me protecting our family. I adore every tough, zealous part of you who will always fight for survivors even if it fucking scares me to think of possibly losing you." He swiped a tear off his cheek. He hadn't even realized he was crying but Winnie had taught him a good man shared his emotions with his family.

Winnie held Joey in her arms and placed Bear's hand on his tummy. "Benton, we'll fight the foe together. Someday we'll look back on this and realize it was just a little valley we had to go through to spend a lifetime in beauty with our family."

Bear nodded. His dad slid his arm around him. "Son, we've got this."

They did. He had to believe his family would solve this. He had a lot of brothers in the MC who would fight until the end to keep his family safe.

Chapter Thirty-One

Bear carried Joey in and had Buttons on a leash until they got into the room. Winnie was helping Phoebe and David bring Zoey in. If they never had to name another animal again, life would be perfect. The kids had finally decided, which was great because the dogs were already doing well with their names. He'd considered leaving the puppies at home but Regina had made it clear everyone was welcome, including all the animals.

As they cleared the door, Scoop took Joey out of his arms and went to sit down at the table. Bear couldn't wait to see his dad's face when he realized Scoop had Joey. He'd overheard the early morning conversation when Locks was feeding Joey. His dad had threatened Locks that since he'd fed him, Joey was all his dad's at lunch.

He turned to help Winnie once he let Buttons off the leash but he was too late. Grant had come over and pulled David away to sit by him. Cannon and Flick were currently trying to convince Phoebe they'd be the better person to sit by. He adored how his family was making his kids feel wanted.

"No, no, no, Cannon. It doesn't matter who Phoebe sits with. She still has to try at least one bite of whatever vegetable is served today."

Phoebe nodded. "Veggies make you run fast and I want to run fast."

"Why do you need to run fast?" Flick questioned, leaning down to hear her answer. Sometimes Phoebe reverted back to a quiet voice when they were in a big group. It was getting better but he could still see her little body getting tense at times.

"Cuz I'm going to work with Mommy and her sisters when I grow up. I'll run fast and shoot straight."

Flick nodded. "I bet you'd be very good at protecting people. Sit by me and I'll show you the veggies I like the best."

Phoebe took Flick's hand and skipped beside him to the table.

"What a brown-nosing little fucker," Cannon whispered.

"Swear jar!" Phoebe yelled, shaking her finger at Cannon with a disappointed look on her face.

"Trust me, she can hear anything." Bear rolled his eyes.

Bear laid his hand against Winnie's back, enjoying his woman and his family getting together for lunch. With so many people wanting to spend time with the kids, he could sit by his woman and bask in the atmosphere without any worries for the moment. He'd decided to compartmentalize the threat to the kids. It was something the therapist had talked about with him. If he couldn't solve it immediately, make a box for it and only pull it out when he was directly working on solving it. It had actually helped a lot.

Baron stood at the front of the table. Everyone quieted waiting for him to say the blessing.

"I promise I won't talk too long because my woman wants everyone to eat her food hot but lately when I look back on what we've built, my heart overflows. The guys and I started Bluff Creek because we were floundering after getting out of the service. We also felt called to make a difference. Now, over forty years later, it's grown beyond my dreams. Adding in all the ways we help change lives makes this old guy so very happy.

So, raise a glass with me to the men and women of the Bluff Creek Brotherhood MC. May we always remember that our greatest triumph is helping those who can't help themselves. Here's to you, my family."

Bear raised his glass, touching Winnie's. Seeing his sunbeam's smiling face and her gorgeous chocolate eyes shining with her love had him wondering why he'd ever doubted if they should be together. He hated what the fire had done but he was grateful it had been the catalyst for him pulling his head out of his ass.

Bear listened to the laughter of his family as he ate. He made sure Winnie had all of her favorites and he even tried the broccoli slaw she brought. He still didn't love the taste of raw broccoli but he wasn't going to undermine teaching their kids to eat healthy.

He'd eaten until he was almost too full. Regina had made fried chicken, mashed potatoes, and gravy. Even though it was on the diner menu and he could have it anytime, it tasted different when Regina cooked it in the MC kitchen. Maybe it was the atmosphere of love the kitchen exuded. He didn't know and didn't care.

"Cane, stop chewing my shoes. Dad will get mad," Grant chastised the puppy.

"It's okay, Grant. I'm sorry I yelled when Cane ate the laces on my boots this morning. He's a puppy and we'll have to teach him to not chew shoes."

"Okay, Dad."

"I'm just glad you found a good name. There was no way I was letting you name your dog *Dog*."

First, one of the sisters giggled. Then Scoop laughed and suddenly the whole room was filled with laughter and giggles.

"What's so fucking funny?"

Voices yelled out, "Swear jar!"

Roam glared around the table. As the laughter died down, Roam was looking at his son.

"Daddy, I really wanted to call him Dog."

"I know, son."

"So Papa got on the computer and looked up what dog was in other languages."

Bear bit his lip, trying to contain his laughter but Roam's face was priceless.

"So Cane is...?"

"Dog in Italian," Baron replied.

Roam shook his head and shoved a bite of food in his mouth. Bear thought him not replying was probably the smartest decision he could have made.

Bear helped clear the table after the meal was done, then smiled with a belly laugh watching Rascal threatening Scoop if he didn't hand over Joey. Scoop stared Rascal in the eye and handed Joey to Sarah.

"What the heck, Scoop?"

"Sarah called dibs way before you walked in the room."

"I'm his Papa, I always have dibs."

Sarah leaned over between Rascal and Scoop. "If you don't want your RV to have major electrical issues the next time you try to watch football, you'll allow me some time with one of my nephews. My house is right by Winnie's. Don't act like you don't see the kids at least three or four hours a day, plus you and Dad do the early morning feeding. It's time you learned to share or else."

Rascal shook his head, stomping off muttering about pushy women. Sarah chuckled and did a little dance as she walked over and settled into one of the recliners near the fireplace. Their MC definitely had strong women who weren't afraid to speak their minds. Rascal may grumble but he had more than once not let one of the sisters hold Joey because they were having Papa time. Bear had known one of the sisters would eventually get fed up and put his dad in his place. Winnie lifted his arm and snuggled up next to him. He leaned over, smelling Winnie's scent that always relaxed him and kissed her hair.

"If you keep smiling so much and laughing, I'm going to wonder where the MC's grumpy S.A.A. went. Did becoming V.P. change your attitude that much?"

He slid his finger under her chin and tilted her face up to reach her mouth. He placed his lips against hers, savoring the feel of her. "Sunbeam, how can I be grumpy when I live with you and our lightning bugs?"

Little arms wrapped around his leg. "Where are the lightning bugs? I want to play with them," Phoebe asked.

He leaned over, slipped his arm under Phoebe's, and settled her on his hip. "Winnie and I have lightning bugs because they flew into our life on Christmas eve and brought their light into our lives. They make me smile and laugh and love and I'm so very happy they're mine."

Phoebe placed her hands against Bear's face, staring into his eyes. "We're your lightning bugs? Me, David, and Joey?"

He nodded, grinning at her perplexed face. "Yep. We never knew how much we needed you in our life. Now with you guys and Winnie, my life is bathed in beautiful, warm light, whether it's during the day or night. I even had Papa Rascal draw up a tattoo of a sun and lightning bugs I'm getting next week."

He heard a sniff over by the tables. He didn't care who heard his words. He'd found what he hadn't known he'd been missing. He kissed Phoebe's button nose, watching her little mouth grin then stretch ear to ear with her smile. "I love you, Daddy and Mommy. Now I gots to go play with the doggies." She bussed his cheek with her lips then wiggled to get down.

He let her down then looked around the room. Even a couple of his brothers were wiping tears away. War walked over, grabbed Bear's elbow, and pulled him in for a hug. Slapping his back a few times, he whispered, "I can't tell you how happy it makes me that you found your one."

Bear hugged War back. So many times over the years, he'd wondered if he and War were both destined to be alone forever but they just had to wait for a while.

Chapter Thirty-Two

Winnie patted Joey's back, then laid him down in the bassinet. She'd love to cuddle him for another couple of hours but she'd brought the kids to the gym with her today. She had paperwork to get done and a couple classes. She'd also put a message into the company's email this morning opening up a position to help with classes either for someone in the MC or security company. If she couldn't find someone inhouse, she'd need to advertise elsewhere.

Winnie checked on Phoebe and David. They'd modified the breakroom next to her office into a play area for the kids. The original breakroom had a small kitchen, self-contained bathroom, tables, chairs, and a TV with a tile floor with one door from her office and one door to the main gym.

The door to the gym had been changed to require a code to get in and could only be opened from inside with the same. They'd pulled out the table and chairs, replacing it with kids' toys, a swing for Joey, a large rug with a racetrack print on it and a play kitchen with child-size chairs and table. Jesse had dropped off a wooden, slanted shelf with books for the kids. A comfy rocker and ottoman was beside a comfy couch. She envisioned having lots of visitors playing with the kids. Why would the gym be any different than their house?

Her watch beeped with a text.

Sarah: Code Rachel at the gym. 11:00 am

Beth: Got it.

Remi: Got it.

Jesse: Finishing Freddy and will be there.

Winnie: Who's Freddy and how are you finishing him?!?!

Jesse: Freddy is the new SUV. I decided since we increased our fleet, they needed names not numbers or letters. Freddy's got the best sound system so you can jam out to Bohemian Rhapsody. I'll bring him so you can properly appreciate him.

Winnie: Does mine have a name?

Jesse: Oh yeah. Rihanna.

Remi: ????

Beth: I get it.

Winnie: You get what?

Sarah: Makes perfect sense. Of course, you've had that song on repeat in the garage at a huge volume. It's good I like that song.

Winnie: What??

Jesse: You know that song Umbrella? That's what you are for Bear and the kids. Plus it's really catchy. In fact, Phoebe and I have been learning a dance to it.

Sarah: It better not be the Tom Holland one.

Jesse: Seriously sometimes I wonder about you guys. C U later.

"Mommy, Joey needs his diaper changed. It's making the room stink."

Guess she'd have to wait to look up what her sisters were talking about. Maybe the kids would help distract her. If Sarah thought she needed emotional backup, it wouldn't be good.

The kids were doing well but after what they'd found out a couple weeks ago, she was constantly waiting for the next bad thing to happen. Although David had Grant to play with, Phoebe didn't have anyone on the compound her age. Winnie would like to enroll Phoebe in school, but she and Bear were both concerned with the safety of the school. It was a joint school between Bluff Creek and another school system that had merged. Although they had a locked door that visitors had to enter through, she was still worried about letting Phoebe out of her sight.

Sarah breezed into her office carrying her computer and a box of pastries before continuing into the kids' area. "Hope you have coffee. I thought we needed a snack."

Winnie followed her in listening to Phoebe tell Sarah all about what they'd been doing. She grabbed the coffee pot, emptying it and rinsing it before she set it to fill. Pulling out the grounds, she dumped them then added a new filter, a scoop and a half of her favorite coffee then shook the salt shaker once. The salt added a smoother flavor and she'd been doing it as long as she could remember. Her mom and Regina both did it to their coffee although Regina added extra cinnamon sometimes.

Remington, Beth, and Jesse walked in with Remington hip-checking Jesse to pick up David first. "Back off, it's my turn to hang out with David. I brought him a new car if he's been good."

David giggled and nodded. "I didn't even cry when Joey's diaper hurt my eyes and nose."

Remington chuckled. "So sorry I missed that. Here you go, buddy." She handed him a 1970 GTO. David had been admiring Grant's and her sister had made sure her son had it, too. She loved the family the kids would grow up in but she was worried—no, petrified. Late at night when she was cuddled with Benton, her mind wouldn't shut off worrying about what Gnat had meant. Although she was anxious to hear what Sarah had found, she'd also rather face a problem than imagine the unknown.

"Okay, so let's grab a cup of coffee, Danish, and meet in the office."

Winnie turned up the show Phoebe and David were watching. "Hey, kiddos, I'm going to shut my door so we don't bother your show. Come get me if you need anything."

"'Kay, Mommy."

Winnie sat down at her desk, leaning back and waiting for whatever bomb Sarah was going to drop. Sarah had her computer hooked into Winnie's larger monitor. She cued up a video.

"Watch this then we'll chat."

Winnie watched the video. It was a conglomeration of multiples videos. Each one showed a large house with a wraparound porch. Gnat went in and out multiple times. She saw different people entering and leaving—mostly men but some women. The outside sign indicated it was a spa. After watching a couple minutes, Sarah paused it then ran it slow as Bear's ex-chief walked in and returned seconds later with a bank bag. Sarah stopped the video then turned to them.

"The teams have identified this is where Gnat works. At first, they assumed she just worked there but the more they watched, they believe she runs the place. When one of our female team members walked in off the street and asked for a spa treatment, she was asked how she found out about them.

When she said she saw the sign, they told her they were a membership only spa."

"Oh, crap," Remington muttered.

"Team one decided to up their surveillance and added listening mics. Clients of the membership spa," Sarah air quoted the words, "gave a code when they went in. From what they have put together the code is what they want and who they want. We authorized whatever means necessary to obtain information. One of the guys noticed an elderly lady who lives behind the house having trouble getting her groceries in. After chatting with her, she's offered her house for us to use for surveillance. She's called the house in numerous times to the police because she's heard screaming and crying. She also identified Gnat as the woman who came over and threatened her if she called it in again."

"So what's the plan beyond surveillance? Are the women there of their own free will or is this a trafficking situation?"

Sarah shook her head. "We don't know yet. Scoop is briefing the guys on this information then we've scheduled a joint meeting this afternoon. This is huge. At last count, the team has identified over fifty individuals who have been to the house more than once."

"Just so you know, we're accepting the offer of using her house as surveillance. She also has a garage with an apartment on top of it that is perfect. We're paying her rent but also upgrading her security. We're pulling in a couple people from the Wichita office so they won't get suspicious. Dad and I have authorized no limit on spending for this. We need to do whatever to keep the kids safe." Remington leaned over when she finished, putting her hand over Winnie's.

Sarah placed her hand over theirs, then Jesse then Beth. Sarah started singing the theme from *Friends*. Remington joined in then the others. Winnie wanted to sing along but she was trying to keep the tears away. Gnat wasn't just a horrible bio-mom, she seemed to be connected. How were they going to keep Winnie's babies safe?

"Winnie, we've got this. We'll hide you and the kids where no one will find you if we think we can't protect you. We'll be there for you, I promise."

Beth's words reminded her she and Bear weren't alone but having to worry about the kids made her furious. Gnat better not come for them. Winnie wasn't going to stand by and allow her to hurt any of them.

Bear smirked at the antics of all the kids, the dogs, and his woman's sisters. Beth had brought all of her dogs to lunch, too.

"The little black dog is Lilly and the Shepherd mix is Dolly. So what's the Schnauzer mix one named?" Cannon was petting the Schnauzer and scratching behind the ears.

"His name is Moss," Beth replied.

Bear had been waiting for this when he'd overheard the women talking about how Beth was going to pay back Cannon for the tinted lotion prank. Bear was positive Cannon wasn't interested in Beth. He had his eye on one of the other sisters. Cannon treated Beth like an annoying little sister. After being in such close quarters with the sisters, Bear had known they'd be paying the guys back for that prank.

"That's my given name."

"Yep." Beth's grin grew and she nodded and popped the P on the word.

"You named your dog after me? Like you knew it was my name?"

Beth chuckled then pointed. "Oh man, this is better than I planned. Yes, Cannon, I fudging know you're the one who put the food dye in my lotion. Plus, let's face it, you're a bit of a hound dog panting after all the women who come to the parties. I thought it was fitting and every time I call his name it makes me smile."

The jeers and laughter from his brothers weren't helping. Bear hadn't ever seen Cannon at a loss for words but the enjoyment was a welcome relief from the tension the last week.

The teams had been watching the house but hadn't been able to get anything concrete besides there were a lot of well-known names visiting it. Winnie had kept him focused on the things they could do like play with the kids and make sure they were adjusting well.

Sarah had been going through Cassidy's boxes from her house. Her last update was she'd found a stack of journals stacked and folded neatly inside a sweater which was then put at the bottom of a trunk. He was curious what the journals contained but right now, there wasn't anything he could do with that. He moved it to the side and put it in his imaginary box. The therapist had given him a list of things to do to cope. When he and Winnie had discussed them, he'd liked Winnie's idea of the box. She used it on security jobs. If it was something that was off or couldn't be taken care of, she'd slide it in what she called her box for later. Then it was off her mind and was on a list to be looked at later. Until Sarah updated them on anything from the journals, they'd remain in the box to be dealt with at a later date.

Phoebe ran over and tugged on Beth's hand. "Can I take Bossy Mossy to play in the play room?"

Beth nodded. "Sure, honey. Remember, if he barks to go outside, come get me?"

"Seriously, Bossy Mossy?"

War chuckled and slapped Cannon on the shoulder. "She's five and she has you pegged, brother."

"Got it. Code Chandler, David."

Bear snickered and then couldn't hold it in, guffawing until tears ran down his face. His five-year-old daughter just used the codes to warn her sibling to not shoot her with the nerf gun as she came in.

Baron walked over with War, shaking their heads. "You are so screwed when she's a teenager. Phoebe is way smarter than all of us and she'll be running everything soon."

"You guys better be ready. We were adding some more codes because we realized we were missing them. She started suggesting stuff from the show. It scares me a little that she watched it because some of the situations are definitely not for kids. We have five new codes we'll be adding and she remembers them all. I wonder if Phoebe has a photographic memory?" Winnie wondered.

Bear could see that because she was constantly amazing him. They had a little memory game and she always won even against him and Winnie. He didn't care what she had. He wanted her to have a wonderful life and do whatever she wanted with it and to do that, they needed to neutralize the threats against them.

Winnie pulled his arm up and snuggled underneath it. "The kids are having fun and the dogs are currently being taken care of. My stomach's full. Maybe we should go take a nap together."

His woman had the perfect idea. Moments alone were few and far between with three kids. Heck, at this point, he'd settle for some heavy petting without being interrupted.

Baron nodded. "Go get some time alone. I'll make sure everyone is covered. At some point, I'd love to hold Joey but Rascal and Locks have been baby hoggers. I shared my grandkids and now that they have some, everything has changed. When War and Remington finally get in gear, their baby is all mine. Not sharing with them."

"Thanks."

Baron's phone sounded and he answered.

Bear decided maybe they should check out one of the new houses they were building. He could grab a blanket and then...

"Bear, we have a sheriff's car with a deputy, a car with the social worker, and another car with one male at the gate requesting to meet with you both."

Baron waited a second, looking at Bear inquiringly. Bear nodded but turned to Cannon. "Can you let her sisters know to keep the kids hidden and quiet?"

Cannon nodded and hurried out of the room.

"Let them in," Baron replied then hung up and walked to open the front door to wait on them. He stood with his arms crossed then jerked.

"Bear, I need you to keep calm. The social worker has your ex-chief with her."

Winnie placed her hand on his chest, rubbing in a circle. "Stay in the moment, Bear. We've got this. In fact, let me lead."

He nodded, letting Winnie know he heard her because he couldn't speak without screaming. He put it in the box like the therapist had suggested but as soon as his ex-chief was gone, he was yanking that fucker out and going through every scenario to keep his family safe.

The social worker passed by Baron and then the ex-chief. He couldn't even appreciate how Baron huffed with disdain as his former boss passed by. Winnie patted his hand then walked toward the social worker, holding out her hand.

"I'm sorry. We didn't expect your visit. Did I miss something on the calendar?"

"No, Ms. Franks, this came up unexpectedly. I know Mr. Carter is familiar with Chief Scott but I don't believe you've met. Chief Scott, this is Winchester Franks, Mr. Carter's fiancée."

Winnie put her hand out to shake. When the chief shook her hand, Bear saw he tightened his grip, trying to make her wince. His woman was strong and didn't show any discomfort on her face.

"What came up unexpectedly? I hope this won't take long. We've had the stomach flu going through the household and one of my sisters just let me know Joey has it now. I'd thought our household had missed it but when kids are together things spread quickly. I want to get him home as soon as possible. Everyone wants to be in the comfort of their homes when they feel under the weather."

The social worker glanced over at the chief. "Well, that changes things. Chief Scott has come forward stating he was dating Cassidy before she died and he believes Joey is his son. We had come to get a sample for DNA but with Joey having the flu, we'll wait."

Bear kept an eye on the chief's face. He was furious his plans had been thwarted but what plans included Joey? The chief was unmarried and he couldn't see him wanting a baby.

"I'm a little confused with this happening now," Winnie commented.

"He just brought it to my attention."

"I know, that's why I'm surprised. Cassidy died in your town. Did you not realize when you worked the crime scene that it was possible he was your son? Why wait until now?"

Chief Scott walked closer to Winnie, his face reddening with his anger. "I was a little busy investigating her death. Now that we've closed the case, I can focus on my son."

Regina walked over closer, squeezing Bear's hand as she walked by. "Oh, I'm so glad to hear that. Who did you arrest?"

Regina's words seemed to add fuel to his anger. Bear waited for the reply because as corrupt as his ex-chief was, he'd be surprised if anyone had been.

"We ruled it a random burglary."

"Hmm." Regina nodded and stared at him, huffing dismissively. Bear had been on the receiving end of that stare along with War and Roam. They'd always broken under her interrogation.

When Regina didn't say anything else, the chief stepped even closer, his belly straining over his belt brushing against her. Baron stood behind him near the door, waiting to see if his woman wanted help.

"What the heck did that mean?"

"I love puzzles and I always pull apart a story until I find all the threads. A random burglary seems a little too easy. Don't you worry. I have plenty of time on my hands. I bet I can help you find who actually committed it."

Regina's threat hung in the air and Bear was positive they all would be pulling threads until they unraveled every little part of Gnat and Chief Scott's life.

"We'll be on our way. Winnie, if you all could, give me a call sometime next week and we can set up a time to do the test.

I'm sure you'll be busy. Phoebe and David have probably been exposed and I don't envy what your little family will be going through for the next few days."

Winnie shook the social worker's hand. "Thank you. I will."

Winnie waited until the door closed. Pulling her watch up to her mouth, she pressed the button. "You get that?"

"Yes, we did, but Phoebe needs you guys immediately."

Bear turned and ran toward the kids' playroom with Winnie at his heels. He skidded to a stop and Cannon moved aside and opened the door to let him pass.

Phoebe was sitting on Sarah's lap, curled as tiny as she could be, crying. Bear bent down and picked her up, cuddling her close with her head in his neck. "Phoebe, what's wrong?"

She shook her head and continued crying. Winnie patted her back, leaning close to Phoebe's ear. "Sweetie, it's okay. Can you tell me why you're sad?"

"Don't let him get me."

Bear breathed deep, keeping his arms from tightening. He was positive he knew who the he was and if he had hurt Phoebe or David, Bear wasn't sure he could keep from taking him out.

"We won't, sweetie. He's gone and you're safe."

Winnie continued patting Phoebe's back as he rubbed up and down. He was missing too many threads. It was time they quit playing defense and went on offense. Chief Scott needed to be removed from the equation. He wasn't sure how yet but by the time they got done planning, he would.

Chapter Thirty-Four

Winnie sipped her hot tea, holding back the tears. They'd gotten the kids back home and settled. Phoebe hadn't wanted Bear to let her go so they'd communicated by text when everyone got together to start planning.

Thank goodness for her sisters. Beth had distracted the sheriff's deputy outside and Jesse had planted three trackers on the chief's car. She figured even if he found one, he'd never find all three. The last one was a special one that she only turned on at different times. Remington, Regina, Cannon, Scoop, and Sarah had divided up the journals and were timelining them on a white board.

Listening to Phoebe whimper until she fell asleep on Bear's shoulder had broken her heart. David had called the chief a bad man but wasn't as upset as Phoebe. He was young enough he might not understand what had happened but he was cuddled up on the bed with both of them. Bear's eyes had been blazing and she'd known if the kids hadn't needed him, he'd be hunting someone down.

The last update had been that War was contacting their Texas chapter for help and also contacting Whiskey and his brothers to see if any of them could help.

Winnie had taken her own insurance out against them losing Joey. She'd texted Cannon that she was worried about their vulnerability behind the house. Bear had snuck in to get her for their date and someone else could do the same. He asked how far she was willing to go. He hadn't answered right away when she said she'd like anyone coming on their property to be obliterated. She was sure he was a little surprised with her answer. She was the sister who always had a smile on her face who ran the gym. She was positive even though she went on security jobs, the guys considered her the least dangerous sister. What they didn't realize is she had a family now and a mother would do anything to protect her children.

He'd finally replied he'd see what he could do. He needed to take into account not compromising the tunnel system and he didn't want any of the deer that were near the property to set it off.

Although she loved her house, maybe they should move into the rooms at her dad's house. With his house being a junction for the tunnel system, there were more options to get away.

Right now, the chief had all the power. He ruled his city and had the mayor in his pocket. They'd identified the mayor as one of the frequent visitors to Gnat's establishment. To get rid of his power, they needed to make it bigger than his city. She texted Remi since she and Sarah were point on the surveillance detail on the house.

Winnie: Has the team been able to get pictures from inside the house?

Sarah: Yes, some aren't usable but Rocky Road is trying to enhance so we can run facial rec.

Winnie: Have him focus on any of the women who look young.

Remi: What are you thinking?

Winnie: If they are minors and crossed state lines then it's a federal case. We've already identified no one new has come in the last week.

Remi: Over state lines and over 24 hours means it could be federal which would negate their power if feds came in.

Sarah: Got it. Mint Chocolate Chip's on it.

Remi: FYI, Whiskey sent Hennesey and a couple cousins to make the rounds at the bars and clubs to see if they could sniff out anything. Hug the kids for us and know we're doing everything we can to keep them safe.

Winnie: Thx

Winnie was thankful they were texting because she wasn't sure she could continue to hold back the tears. She was frustrated, angry and so very scared. What if they couldn't keep the kids safe? The biggest and baddest didn't always win and sometimes innocents were hurt.

Bear's warm arms wrapped around her as she gazed out the window. He took the cup out of her hand and placed it on the counter. His finger tilted her chin so he could see her.

"You've been so strong today, Sunbeam." His kissed her lips. Not a sexual one where he wanted to claim her. A kiss promising he'd go through this with her. He pulled back and she buried her face in his chest, letting the first sob break free, her hands holding tight to his cut. She tried to muffle her sobbing because she didn't want to wake Phoebe up and worry her.

Bear's hand held the back of her head and his voice whispered in her ear. "You've always been my sunbeam, always sharing your light with everyone else, but even the sun gets overpowered by the clouds sometimes."

She cried for the kids who would never get to be held in Cassidy's arms again and she cried because she worried she wouldn't get to always hold the kids. Her Benton just held her, kissing her hair and being her shelter when she couldn't hold herself up.

"So, you're going to cry all the tears you need to. I'm going to be like that song you were singing the other day. I'll be your umbrella when the rain comes and then we're going to rip into their lives, examine everything and find where they are vulnerable. Then we're going to do whatever it takes to make sure those kids are always part of our family."

She could live with that. "Let's go snuggle with the kids in bed. I need to hold them."

Bear kissed her forehead. "You go on ahead. I'm going to check the doors after I let Rascal in. He's taking first watch on the couch. Locks is going to relieve him at four. Tomorrow we can discuss where the safest place is for our family."

Chapter Thirty-Five

They'd decided not to move into Locks' house. Cannon and Scoop had completed some security additions for the time being. Bear was pushing for a new development in the middle of the new property. He and Winnie had started writing down what they wanted in a house. He figured Winnie was the most excited about the new housing area—besides providing more security, it would also have her minutes from the gym.

It had been a week of ups and downs. His worry had grown over the last week of when the next hit might come. After discussing with Winnie the ramifications over Joey's DNA test, Roam had offered the perfect solution. They'd sent a sample of Grant's saliva in. The test would return that the chief wasn't the father and Joey would be safe with them. With the backup at the lab where the state did testing, their social worker had said it would be at least four weeks, possibly longer.

He and his family would do anything to keep Joey out of the chief's hands even if it meant submitting false information.

The journals had been gone through but Sarah and Scoop had said they didn't want to share anything until they had confirmation on a couple of items. Today's meeting in the clubhouse was for an update. Regina would be watching the kids along with a couple of prospects. His daughter was pouting because he'd said no to bringing the puppies. Regina was more than happy to have them but with so many people in the meeting, he didn't want to have someone's time taken to let the puppies outside.

"Hmmmph." Phoebe huffed as he opened her door. He was sure he wouldn't find this adorable when she was sixteen but seeing his little five-year-old glaring at him with her arms crossed had him fighting a grin.

"Let's go inside. I heard Regina say she needed you all helping her frost cinnamon rolls."

His daughter's face perked up a little but then she scrunched her forehead. "I'll help cuz I love cinn'mon rolls but I'm still angry with you."

He nodded his head. "I know but sometimes dads have to do what is best for the family. Sometimes I have to say no."

He leaned down and brushed a kiss against her head, giving her a hug. She squirmed out of his arms and ran toward the front door, David following behind her.

Scoop laughed as he unbuckled Joey. His woman had taken the snacks and diaper bag for Joey in. "She's got quite the personality. It makes me happy for you, Bear, that she knows how much you all love her. She feels comfortable showing her anger."

"Oh, yeah she does. After I told her no at the house, she went in and talked to the puppies. Loud enough I could hear her."

"What she'd say?"

"Oh, how she loved them but Daddy was in a bad mood and she was sorry he wouldn't let them come. Then she told Buttons if he didn't straighten up and quit chewing boots, Daddy might not let him sleep in David's bed."

Bear held the door as Scoop walked through where Locks immediately took Joey out of his arms.

"Seriously?"

"Be careful, Mint Chocolate Chip. Ice cream melts under heat." Locks' glare backed up his word.

"No, no, no. You all are not calling me anything but Scoop." Scoop stomped off toward their council room, holding his hand above his head and saluting Locks with one finger.

They might fight over holding Joey but they fought just as much over getting time with the little kids. Baron walked out and handed a piece of fabric to Locks.

"Nice. How many did she make?"

Locks handed Joey to Baron. "Hold him just a second. No taking him away."

Locks picked up the fabric, efficiently wrapping it around him until it formed a sling. He lifted Joey out of Baron's arms, gently placing him in the wrap, situating him.

"She made two for each of you to have so you could have one being washed. They're all personalized with the Brotherhood's insignia."

If Bear had any doubt about the dedication of the Papas, this would dissuade them. Personalized baby slings so they could carry around his son. He smiled and headed into council. Winnie had an open space beside her that he quickly grabbed. It might be a serious meeting but his brothers had no problem taking the seat to mess with him.

"Okay, everybody's here so let's get started. Scoop, Sarah, Beth, this is all your show. Who's starting?"

Sarah took a breath then started. "Cassidy wrote everything down. We're guessing the journals are what whoever trashed her place was looking for. We've discussed how to tell you and honestly, guys, there's no easy way. We're going to lay it out for you and at any time, you can ask us to pause for questions."

Bear nodded, reaching for Winnie's hand. None of this sounded good and he had a feeling he'd only get through this holding onto his sunbeam.

"About five years after Gnat left here, she ended up being picked up for prostitution by none other than Chief Scott. Charges were dropped. We think at this time is when they came up with the idea of building something together. They lived together and Gnat became pregnant, delivering a little girl she named Cassidy."

Bear jerked. "What? She was my half-sister?"

Winnie held his hand, turning toward him to rub his chest. He looked in her eyes. How could she still have the love shining out of her eyes when he'd let his sister down?

"Yes. Although from what we can tell, she didn't know she had a brother. Ten years later, Gnat had another daughter, given name Kennedy. It's our assumption Chief Scott is the father to both, although the father's name was left blank on both certificates, but it's what Cassidy believed."

Sarah paused until Bear nodded. He wasn't okay by any means but they needed to get through this. Scoop took over, throwing a picture up on the screen.

"Cassidy and Kennedy both attended school through their sophomore years. At this point, Cassidy indicated they were expected to join the family business. Cassidy joined when she was seventeen under duress. She was put into what she called the spa's stable."

"Hold up, so her parents made her become a prostitute?" Winnie's voice held the disbelief he'd expect from someone who'd had loving parents. With his experiences with Gnat, he was surprised she'd hadn't forced Cassidy earlier.

Scoop nodded, continuing. "What we can't figure out and Cassidy didn't understand was anyone else in the stable who became pregnant was required to get an abortion. Cassidy wasn't. Kennedy joined when she was seventeen under the same conditions as Cassidy. For a while, they lived together. In fact, Kennedy babysat a lot when Cassidy had Phoebe. For some reason, everything changed when David was around six months."

Scoop nodded at Sarah to take over. "Kennedy was moved into the spa full-time. Cassidy's journal speculates Gnat was worried they'd run. She was allowed to watch Cassidy's kids but only at the spa. Cassidy was sent to work the streets instead of the spa. There is a huge gap in the journals. We're not sure if she just quit writing or if we're missing one. It picks up when you leave town and bring her the money. She's thankful and believes you're the nicest man she'd ever met, only wanting to help her and not expecting anything in return."

Bear realized his face was wet when Winnie used a tissue to wipe the tears off his cheeks. He didn't want to ask the question but he had to know. "Did she know we were siblings?"

Sarah shook her head. "No. You were just a really nice man. She wanted to take you up on the offer to come to Bluff Creek but she couldn't figure out how to get Kennedy free, too."

Beth took over. "Two weeks before Cassidy died, she went to the courthouse and asked how to update a birth certificate. We think this is what triggered her attack. When she was told it would require she and the father to both complete forms and appear before a judge, she left. She wrote she then checked with a social worker in DCS. She indicated she was concerned what would happen to her kids. The DCS worker showed her how to complete an online will. Cassidy wrote she added your name as father for the kids in handwriting on the form. She was planning on getting in her car and just driving her and the kids here."

Rascal walked over behind Bear, placing his hand on his shoulder. Beth had paused but continued at Rascal's nod. Her eyes filled with tears then she swallowed. "Sorry, this is hard to tell you. The timeline was upped when Kennedy overhead Gnat talking with the chief about how much money they could make if they sold Joey. Infants were in high demand and that infuse of cash could help them expand."

Bear let go of Winnie's hand and pounded his fists on the table to release enough anger he could focus. Winnie's voice in his ear brought him back.

"We will never let them have him. We'll keep him safe. We've got this. Now channel that anger, my wonderful analytical man. We need your expertise to help plan for how we're going to do this."

His listened to her calm voice, though he could hear the anger underlying every word she said. He leaned back and nodded for them to continue. Beth wiped her nose and shook her head, motioning for Scoop to continue.

"Her last entry is that she'd put the kids to bed and was going to go to bed, wake at three a.m. and leave for here. She had complete faith that once she got here, Bear and his friends would keep her kids safe while she went back for Kennedy. The date coincides with the night she died. We're guessing the kids would have just disappeared, never to be seen again, but the next-door neighbors you'd asked about watching over her called it in and waited with the kids until the social worker came. The older woman who lived to the west said the chief had tried to get her to go home before someone from the department of children's services showed up. I'm positive she saved those kids."

Bear turned to his sunbeam. Her face was a little fuzzy because he couldn't seem to stop crying. If only he'd known he had sisters, he would have never allowed them to go through this. His kids would know someday what a brave mother they'd had but right now, he had to get himself under control and help figure out how to rescue his other sister. He didn't care whether they were half-siblings. Once they rescued her, they'd get her help and let her become the person she was meant to be.

Winnie nodded, leaning her forehead against his, tears falling down her face.

"I want her to live with us. I want her to have family around her and I want the kids to get to enjoy their aunt."

"Anything you want. She deserves a family that loves her and we'll be that."

Chapter Thirty-Six

Over the years, Locks had built up a network of contacts in all the big agencies. It had taken two weeks but they'd put a plan in place. It had become a federal case when two of the girls were identified from pictures as being fifteen and from Texas and Oklahoma. They'd both been missing for over a year. Locks' contact in the FBI and one in the DEA had allowed the security company to provide backup. Unfortunately, they'd been told to remain as backup only.

Originally Bear had wanted to have both Gnat and the chief vanish from the face of the earth but then Winnie and her sisters had talked with him. Jesse had gone over how old they both were and how many years they probably had left. Then she'd gone into all the things that might happen to them in the federal system when people knew they trafficked in kids. Her argument for a lifetime of suffering instead of a quick bullet to the head had convinced him.

Bear, Winnie and Beth were here along with a decent amount of the security company and MC. The kids were safe at home with Remi, Regina, Sarah and Jesse along with the originals. They decided to make it an adventure for the kids and something special. The sisters and a couple of the brothers had decorated in the tunnel closest to Locks' house, making it a camping wonderland with tents, sleeping bags, a flameless fire they could make s'mores on and a huge screen for their movies. Glow-in-the-dark stars had been added to the ceiling of the tunnel. His family was as safe as they could be.

The feds had confirmed that Gnat and the chief were both in residence tonight. He and the sisters were in the command van waiting to be called in if needed, or when Kennedy was found.

Breach in 3, 2,1 came through the sound. There were multiple screens on the helmet cams. He followed Winnie's finger pointing at screen two. Gnat was fighting a couple of officers, not complying with their orders to get on the floor. What did it say about their lack of relationship that he didn't feel anything as the four officers wrestled her to the floor, employing a taser to get her to comply? She'd not only failed as a mother but willingly sold her children. He hoped she rotted in jail and experienced everything she'd done to others.

Winnie's fingers laced through his, giving a small squeeze. His sunbeam would always have his back and their kids'. He wasn't sure what they'd be dealing with but he and his sunbeam would help Kennedy however she needed.

Bear's attention turned to another screen as gunfire sounded in one of the rooms. There were so many people in the room, all the camera was currently showing were the backs of the officers.

"Target two apprehended. We're going to need a bus as soon as scene is secured."

"Shit, Ellie. Did you mean to shoot off his dick? Remind me not to tick you off."

"Officer Howard, your mic is hot. Keep your comments to yourself."

Winnie was smothering a grin and her eyes were dancing. He was sure his face looked the same. He'd need to find this Ellie and give her a medal. He couldn't think of a finer thing to happen to the now ex-chief. He scanned the screens, hoping to see Kennedy alive in them.

"Scene secure. Send in medics. Subject One has been found and is alive. Bringing her out now."

They'd found Kennedy and she was alive. He wasn't sure if that meant she wasn't hurt or was just able to walk on her own. He'd lost one sister. He wasn't letting this one away. Winnie grabbed his hand and pulled him out the door. He loved that his sunbeam was as anxious to see Kennedy as he was. They wound their way through the support personnel who had moved closer once the scene was secure.

Bear paused when an officer walked out with Kennedy beside him. He catalogued her injuries—a black eye and some scrapes but she was walking on her own. He didn't know what to do. Did she know she had a brother? Would she hate him for not rescuing her earlier? He wasn't sure how he'd handle it if she refused to come with them.

Kennedy was looking around the area with personnel all over. The officer with her motioned his head toward Bear and walked her over. She paused when she was in front of him.

"Is it true you're my brother and even though you knew nothing about me, you worked to get me rescued?"

Winnie waited to see if Bear needed her to step in. Kennedy and he were just staring at each other after her question.

"I swear to you, if I'd known she had you or Cassidy, I would have gotten you out sooner." Bear's gruff voice whispered the words as tears ran down his cheeks.

Kennedy's eyes filled and then she threw her arms around Bear, burying her head in his chest. "Thank you."

Winnie stood close, letting them have their moment until a screech rent the air.

"You! I should have drowned you both at birth."

Kennedy's head raised and she untangled herself from Bear's arms. "Just a sec. Need to do something."

Kennedy strode over to Gnat who was held between two officers. Bear followed right behind and Winnie stayed close. She was okay with someone hitting Gnat but didn't want Bear to lose control and have an officer think they needed to stop him.

Kennedy paused in front of the trio. "You know. There's something I've always wanted to say to you."

"Oh, now that he's here, you think you're special? Go on, say it, trash. Don't get too comfortable. I'll be out on bail soon."

"I think you need to get that last plastic surgery fixed. It's a little off."

Kennedy punctuated her last word with a right hook to Gnat's face, knocking her head back.

"You bitch. You broke my nose. Aren't you going to do something?"

One of the officers laughed while the other looked at Kennedy and nodded his head. "Nice right hook. You telegraphed your move with your feet. You might work on that."

They pulled their charge toward one of the vans they'd brought to transport prisoners with her screeching the whole way. Two EMTs came out the front door of the spa with a gurney in between them and the now ex-chief cuffed to the gurney. Two feds walked with him. A female officer walked behind with what Winnie was guessing her supervisor yelling at her.

"Seriously, Ellie. I know you're a good shot so don't try to convince me you didn't mean to shoot his dick off. Do you know the type of liability you've opened the department to? I'm not sure if you're a good fit to our team."

Oh, if that asinine man thought he was going to scream at the woman who Winnie wanted to give a medal to, he was mistaken. Winnie walked away from Bear and Kennedy, stopping right in front of the stairs so the two would have to stop. Beth joined her.

The man paused griping at Ellie when they stepped off the last stair. "Can I help you? You don't have identification. How the hell did you get on the property?"

Winnie ignored his questions, instead looking Ellie in the eye. "I want to thank you for giving the chief just a taste of what he deserved. I help run my family's bail bonds and security company. We appreciate initiative and I guarantee we also pay well above what you're making working for him. You'd be a perfect fit for our team and I can see you leading teams. We have offices all over so you wouldn't even need to relocate if you didn't want to. Honestly, though, I'd love to have you at our main offices in Bluff Creek. Consider this your formal offer if you want to work for a company who values initiative and will never demean your contribution."

"Listen, you… Hey, Officer, get this woman off the property." He punctuated his words with a finger poking her chest. Winnie grabbed his finger, twisting it until she was positive he'd gotten her point then let it go.

"We also don't allow people to touch others without their consent, which I believe your boss has yet to learn. Franks and Daughters Bail Bonds in Bluff Creek if you want a job. Ask for Winchester Franks. I run our gym."

Winnie turned to go and the man tried to grab her arm but Beth stepped between them, catching his hand. "You may not know who we are but your boss does. So I'll reiterate what my sister just said. We don't allow people to touch others without their consent. Keep your paws to yourself or you won't like what happens."

Winnie turned back at Beth's words. She'd always watch her sisters' backs even though Beth was fully capable of dealing with this douche nozzle.

"Are you threatening me?"

Beth laughed. "I prefer the word promise. Ellie, I'm Beth, and I'd love to have you work with us. I do surveillance which is way more fun than the gym. I could always use a partner."

Winnie turned toward her man and his newly found sister, leaving Beth to chat with Ellie. The happiness on Bear's face warmed her heart. His eyes flashed with approval at her speaking her mind. She walked over and opened her arms. "Can I hug my new sister? I'm Winnie, this one's fiancée."

Kennedy nodded and opened her arms. Winnie wrapped her arms around Kennedy, feeling the shudders work through her. "I can't wait for you to come home with us."

Bear's arms wrapped around both of them, his unique scent bringing her peace despite the noise around them. Gnat and the chief were in custody. Kennedy was with them and they could move on.

"Hey, Winchester. If you're serious, I'll turn in my notice and be there in two weeks."

Winnie pulled away a little. "You bet. Beth can give you all the information."

They'd helped bring down two people who had not only hurt her man but so many others and picked up a new employee. If she did say so herself, it had been a fantastic day.

Chapter Thirty-Seven

Winnie had dropped the kids off at the clubhouse. Regina had organized a kids' sleepover to welcome Ellie and her kids. When Beth had told them about Ellie's situation, they hadn't wasted any time in helping her get moved. That woman had a story to tell but Winnie didn't have time to worry about that right now.

The sisters had all decided with the number of kids on the property, a permanent daycare was a necessity. They'd already put the call in to Bluff Creek Brotherhood Construction to add on the daycare to the list of construction projects along with the new houses being built. She'd miss her house when they moved but with Kennedy coming to Bluff Creek, they needed more room.

She and Bear had met with the social worker. They had official things that needed to happen but the social worker seemed to think it would all go smoothly. She'd mentioned having them married would help the process, too. She wanted to be married but Remi got engaged first. She didn't want to overshadow her sister but then Remi had pulled her aside. Remi wanted her version of a big biker wedding with Locks walking her down an aisle lined by motorcycles outside on the property. She'd have to wait for warmer weather.

Remi had asked the hard question. What exactly did Winnie want? She wanted her man by her side and to be married. The getting there part didn't matter to her as long as their kids were there. They'd done everything out of order so why should it change now?

She and Remi had put out a Code Rachel and everyone had met in Sarah's office. They'd called Regina and explained what Remi wanted later and what Winnie wanted to do now as soon as it was possible. Regina and Baron were friends with a retired judge who lived about twenty miles away outside Coldwater. If Winnie would get the license then Regina would have the judge at Sunday lunch to perform the ceremony. They'd wear what they wanted and the guys could, too. For Winnie, it wasn't about the event—it was about tying her life to Benton's permanently.

She was hoping he was home because she couldn't wait to spend a little alone time with her man. Unlocking the door, she hung up her jacket and listened. The puppies were asleep in their crate and music was playing quietly from their bedroom.

"Bear, you here?"

She walked to the doorway and was struck speechless at the sight before her. Bear was leaned against the headboard, his legs cocked open. The sunlight coming through the blinds highlighted every delicious inch of her man, tattoos and all. His hand was sliding up and down his hard cock. His white teeth smiled between his dark beard. She wasn't sure where to look first because his body was a feast for her eyes. Hard planes, smooth muscles and so many places she wanted to lick.

"Sunbeam, how about you lose those clothes and crawl up here? I think for getting our wedding planned, you deserve a reward."

Of course he already knew when they were getting married. Her dad had been outside the room when they called Regina. Those men gossiped worse than anyone she knew.

She wasted no time removing her clothes and tossing them on the chair. She'd worry about wrinkles later. She placed her hands on the bed, then crawled up Bear, kissing his knee, then his thighs, pointedly ignoring his weeping cock.

"What's my reward?"

He chuckled, sliding down the bed until her pussy was hovering on his chest and her nipples were above his mouth. He leaned up, nibbling then sucking until he had her undulating against his chest before answering.

"As tantalizing as those are, I want you to move up here and sit on my face. I plan to eat your pussy until you scream."

Until she screamed sounded perfect. Two nights ago, Benton had to flip her over and plow into her from behind. She'd had to muffle her screams in the pillow because her man gave it to her that good. Not having to stay quiet let her concentrate on Benton and how he made her feel.

"Come on, Sunbeam. Scootch up here."

His hands grasped her thighs, lifting to move her until she scooted. She reached for the headboard because hovering over him felt awkward.

"Babe, my tongue's not that long. Come closer."

She would but what if she smothered him? Yeah, she was lean because she ran but still, if her pussy cut off his air to his nose, he'd die.

"Benton, how about we just make love?"

"All in good time, Sunbeam." His gruff voice did things to her and she tried to squeeze her thighs around him to stop the ache.

His hands grasped her thighs tighter and pulled her down to his mouth. His lips and tongue started lightly licking then her man dove in, feasting on each hill and crevice of her pussy. She was glad she had her hand on the headboard to keep upright. Bear found that perfect spot and was relentlessly driving her up. He started to pull away and she grasped his hair, directing him back to that spot. The one that had her trembling and lights flashing behind her eyes.

His tongue worked her along with his finger rubbing inside her with a come-hither movement. Suddenly she was screaming his name and not caring if he could breathe. She shuddered as she came down. Bear's hands helped her slide down his body then he was rolling them over.

"You are fucking beautiful, Sunbeam, and so hot when you come. I need inside you or I'll blow on the sheets."

He punctuated his words with a long, slow glide in then started hammering his cock into her. His hands pulled her legs up on his hips and she held onto his arms. Benton's eyes blazed with heat. She'd never get tired of seeing him above her, reminding her how much he loved her. She wrapped her legs around this hips, crossing her ankles, changing the angle.

"Oh fuck, Sunbeam." Her legs wrapped around his waist was Benton's kryptonite. He loved the angle but so did she. She'd thought she'd just enjoy watching her man but he knew what he was doing. His fingers sliding between them and rubbing her clit had her skyrocketing up. Two erratic thrusts and Benton was groaning his release and she was following him. When she dreamed of a life with her faceless one back before she fell for Benton, she'd never grasped how deep her love would be. He'd been the missing part of her life and now she had him and a whole life. She couldn't wait for it to be official.

Chapter Thirty-Eight

Lunch was almost over. His sunbeam was going to be his officially. It was good the sisters had helped with the kids this morning because it had allowed him to sneak away and have his little project done. A small part of the wrap showed underneath his t-shirt but he'd kept a sweatshirt on at lunch under his cut. He planned on taking off the sweatshirt before they started.

"The judge will be here in a couple minutes. Let's get this stuff cleaned up so we can make room." Regina directed everyone while Bear grabbed David and nodded at Rascal to grab Joey. He motioned for Scoop to slip Phoebe away, too. He had the items Sarah had been working on. What Winnie did realize is it helped having friends in high places. All the red tape had been moved out of the way with their help in the trafficking arrests. As soon as he and Winnie were married, they'd sign their names and the judge would witness. The kids were taking his and Winnie's last name.

Kennedy had been staying with Jesse in her house. When their house was done it would have plenty of room for her to move into it with them. He'd been spending time getting to know her even though it was a little awkward at times. She'd started seeing the same therapist he did and it seemed to be helping.

He leaned down and showed Phoebe her jacket. Since the girls had already had the idea for embroidered jean jackets, he'd just had Sarah add a couple of things when she was working on them. In addition to the Bluff Creek Brotherhood MC on them, he'd had her add Bear's Lightning Bugs. Phoebe smiled then jumped up and down. He'd known when he asked Sarah to do the stitching in purple his girl would adore it. She slipped her arms into the jacket then threw them around his neck.

"I love you, Daddy. I'll always be your lightning bug even when I get to catch the bad guys."

He fought back tears. This girl had his heart and he had no doubt she'd catch bad guys when she grew up.

"I love you, too. Now, let me help David."

He turned to David and held out his jacket. He'd chosen the traditional black, burgundy and gray their emblem had. David slipped it on, rubbing his fingers along the stitching. "I gots one like Grant."

"Yep, because you're a part of my family and a part of the club. I love you, David."

"Love you, Daddy. Hurry, I wants to show Grant."

Bear turned to see Rascal had slid Joey's jacket on him. "Son, let's go get you married."

Rascal patted him on the back then Bear walked out holding both kids. Winnie stood at the front of the room by the fireplace. In the time he'd been gone, they'd draped the mantel in a greenery rope with candles interspersed and black and burgundy ribbons. Winnie waited beside the judge in her jeans, motorcycle boots and long-sleeve shirt with her property cut. Her smiled widened when she saw the kids' jackets.

He walked up to the woman who had brought the sunshine into his life and given him a family. "You ready to do this?"

She nodded. "I've been waiting for this for fourteen years, Benton."

The judged nodded.

Winnie held David's hand with her right hand and laid her left on Benton's hand which was cuddling Joey. Phoebe held David's hand and also Bear's. The kids were just as much a part of this as she and Benton were.

"Winchester Franks and Benton Carter have chosen to pledge their lives together. Benton?"

"I take you, Winchester Franks, as my lawful wife and pledge I will honor and love you until the last breath leaves my body."

Winnie swallowed and hoped she could get through her vows before she choked up too much. She'd waited too long for this and she was finally getting everything she'd fought for.

"I take you, Benton Carter, as my lawful husband and pledge I will honor, love and remind you how very special you are to us until the last breath leaves my body."

"You may kiss the bride."

Benton leaned over, claiming her lips for the first time as husband and wife. It was too short but having kids, she realized it was a norm now.

"Now, this is a joyous day because we not only celebrate the wedding of Benton and Winchester, but we're celebrating them joining their lives officially with the children Phoebe Lisa, David Ross and Joey Matthew. Now, all the official stuff is taken care of but I want to ask Phoebe and David, do you want to have Benton and Winchester as your mommy and daddy forever and ever?"

Winnie could hear multiple sniffles from their family. David nodded but Phoebe leaned over and whispered in his ear. His face scrunched up and he shook his head at her. She widened her eyes and nodded her head. He shook his head then turned to the judge.

"Yes, foreva." David leaned his head against her leg.

The judge hid a smile then waited on Phoebe.

"Yes, I want them forever but I hoped we could get an adoption present out of it."

Laughter spilled out of the guests. When they'd quieted enough, the judge continued.

"By the power of the state of Kansas, I announce to you the Carter family."

Yells, whoops, and clapping filled the room.

Winnie breathed a sigh of relief. She and Benton were officially married and the kids were theirs. Benton handed her Joey then pulled his sleeve up. He got down on one knee so the kids could see. Winnie bent down because she wanted to see, too.

"Remember I told you how Mommy brought the sun into my life and then you, my little lightning bugs, brought light, too?"

Phoebe and David nodded. "Well, I decided besides having you in my life, I wanted to always carry you around with me no matter where we're at." Benton turned his arm so they could see his new tattoo. "See, here's Mommy and here are all of you, the little lightning bugs circling the sun."

Benton caught both the kids as they threw their arms around him. His face turned toward her, his eyes full of tears. He mouthed thank you to her but he didn't realize she owed him the thanks. Sure, she'd chased him but he had to be willing to face his past so they could be whole together. She'd always be thankful for her man's soft center filled with love for his family.

Chapter Thirty-Nine

Winnie finished the last curl in Phoebe's hair then handed her the mirror so she could see the back of her hair. Remington had wanted them all matching so Phoebe had a miniature version of the bridesmaids dress with her jean jacket on. The rest of the bridesmaids had the dress on. Remi and she were the only ones with the property cuts on, though.

Bear and she had been married three months. Phoebe was attending school and doing great. The construction was scheduled to be started on the daycare within the Franks offices and Sarah would be overseeing hiring people when it was finished. Their house and Remi and War's had been completed. While Remi and War went on a short honeymoon, both households would be moved.

Kennedy had decided to live with them for awhile since they'd made her a suite with a separate entrance but was still part of the house. She was figuring out what exactly she wanted to do. She'd been attending therapy and working through her issues. Winnie personally thought she had a serious admirer as often as he visited their house but Kennedy wasn't sharing.

Winnie looked at her gorgeous older sister. Who knew when they were decorating War's bike where it would lead to? Remi's dress was a stunning white A-line silhouette with a black lace bodice overlay. The skirt was an asymmetrical white satin with a black lace underlay edge.

Her only motorcycle boot sister had fallen in love with silver heeled sandals while they were shopping. She had her property cut over the dress and was carrying a small bouquet of the same flowers War had brought her on their first date. Remi might be tough but she was sentimental, too. Winnie couldn't wait until Remi had her man and everything she'd always wanted.

They lined up. They were walking down the aisle alone, War waiting at the front. All the other guys were sitting on their motorcycles which lined the aisle. She wondered who would win. The MC guys had all wanted to rev their motorcycles as she walked down the aisle. Remi had wanted to walk in to music and then have the guys rev the motorcycles at the end.

The music started and she giggled. Beth was first then Jesse then her. Only her sister would have them walk in to the *Friends* theme song. Bear was grinning as she passed him on his motorcycle, blowing her a kiss. As she passed Rascal, she saw he'd won who got to hold Joey during the ceremony. It's not like Locks could walk with Remi down the aisle and hold Joey. Her dad still planned to live in the main house. With them relocating, her dad would no longer be able to see when their lights went on. She was sure there would be an adjustment. Grant, David and Phoebe were the ring bearers and flower girl. Kennedy was in charge of having them sit by her once they were done.

She took her place and then Sarah followed quickly. The music stopped. Winnie waited to see what Remington had picked. She'd kept quiet and hadn't shared. The first strains of the music started and she smiled. Bryan Adams' "Everything I Do, I Do It for You" played as Remington walked through with her arm through Locks'.

War's face brightened when he caught sight of her sister but what made Winnie smile was her man's eyes on her. He mouthed I love you and she teared up. She would never take for granted the love she and her husband shared. They'd fought too hard for it.

Sarah watched Remington and War on the dance floor the MC had constructed under the stars. The drinks were flowing and everyone was celebrating. Things had calmed down some and now she could concentrate on what she wanted.

She loved her job and her family but she wanted more. She wanted to bake the cookies, take her kids to school and have her husband come home to a homemade dinner. She wouldn't give up her job but she wanted more. She wanted what her sisters had—men who adored them and completed them.

Her eyes drifted to the man who was entirely too young for her but she couldn't keep off her mind. He was wicked smart, had a fantastic sense of humor and his body had her reaching for her battery-operated boyfriend so many nights.

They worked fantastic together so there was so much to lose if she acted on her desires. What if he didn't feel the same and thought she was just an older woman coming onto him? Plus, she wasn't like her sisters body wise. She had some major junk in the trunk and her breasts were way more than a handful. She enjoyed baking and sampling her baking and despite Winnie pushing her to work out, she did the bare minimum to keep qualified for their jobs. She hated sweating.

Let's face it. If she was running, there was a darn good reason. Either she was chasing someone or something, or someone was chasing her.

Maybe she'd go drown her sorrows at the bar. It's not like she was driving home and maybe, just maybe, she could forget about him for one night.

Scoop kept an eye on the woman he'd been falling for. Straight up head over heels, he couldn't imagine ever being happy without her. Add in the fact that no matter what woman was around or how skimpily she was dressed, he didn't get hard. Nope, his dick only perked up when she was around. And man, when she leaned over him to point out something on the computer, her hair falling across his shoulder smelling of vanilla, the fucker turned hard as steel. And if she had her hair up in a messy bun on top of her head and her computer glasses on, his dick thought it was time to play ravish the hot librarian.

Too bad there were two things wrong with that scenario. First, he was positive he was in her friend zone. Being friends with the woman he couldn't get off his mind was a great start but it wasn't where he wanted to stay. And second, he had zero experience ravishing a woman. A thirty-five-year-old virgin that hadn't even had a blow job. He didn't have any special reason. When he would have been going out in high school and later college, he was helping to raise his younger twin sisters and working two part-time jobs for food on their table to help his mom out after their dad had left. Then he was focused on getting into the police academy. Once he finally had some time to himself, he hadn't connected with anyone. If he'd waited that long to finally take care of his pesky virginity, he didn't want to just bang one out in a bar bathroom, though if she gave him the time of day, he'd do it anywhere.

Cannon was across the room talking to her. Scoop had never wanted to hit one of his friends more than when she laughed at something he said, tucking her hair behind her ear. Scoop was positive Cannon wasn't interested in her but he envied the easy way Cannon flirted.

She was the whole package—brains, an hourglass figure he wanted to explore and a personality that had him craving her presence.

Flick tapped him on the shoulder. "When are you going to make your move?"

Scoop shook his head, tossing back another drink. He wasn't sure what number drink it was but everything was getting nice and fuzzy. Fuzzy helped because then it didn't hurt so much if she ignored him. At least he only had to walk down the hallway if he drank too much. "She thinks I'm a friend. She doesn't see me like that."

Flick sipped his beer then tilted the bottle toward her. "Then build on that. Friends, then friends with benefits. You could ask her to help you with a favor. Getting rid of a certain status you have. Then when she falls for all the deliciousness of Mint Chocolate Chip, slip a ring on her finger and walk her down the aisle before she comes out of the sex daze."

Flick was a prankster and Scoop wasn't sure if he was serious or not. He might like her calling him that but no one else was allowed. He was fine with the name Scoop. They wouldn't be changing it to any of the ice cream flavors she called him.

"Are you joking or really suggesting I should do that?"

Flick laid his hand on Scoop's shoulder. "Man, you've been falling for her since the first time you all collaborated on tech stuff. Think about this—do you want to be her friend and then maybe watch someone else romance her or do you want to go after the woman who puts a look on your face I've never seen before?"

He nodded, then swallowed. His mouth was dry and his heart pounded loud enough his chest felt like he was near the speakers at a rock concert. He licked his lip then decided to hell with it. The worst that could happen is she'd say no. He grabbed another drink, downed it then nodded at the bartender to set him up again. He needed a little liquid courage for this, or maybe a whole lot of liquid courage. Quickly downing the next two, he decided it was now or never. He couldn't live with never. He weaved over to where Sarah was standing. Cannon had walked away.

"Could I talk to you about something?"

Sarah didn't answer right away, gazing into his eyes. She must have found the answer she needed because she nodded. She headed to the side of the yard, closer to the orchard entrance. He followed behind her, trying to enjoy the sight of her rounded bubble butt cupped by her bridesmaids dress, but he was focusing on putting one foot in front of the other and not throwing up.

She paused at the entrance to the orchard. "What do you need?"

What did he need? He needed to cup her face in his hands, lay his lips against her and claim her. He wanted to see if she tasted as good as she smelled.

"I need to know if you'd be willing to help me with something."

Sarah smiled at him. Why did his heart feel better when she smiled? They could be frustrated and searching for a thread of information. She'd smile and bam, everything was better.

"Sure, if I can. Whatcha need, Rocky Road?"

"It's a huge favor but you're the only one I'd consider."

"Okay. I'll help you with whatever I can."

Yeah, he needed her help and if she would, he'd take anything. He stepped closer, sliding his arm around her waist, fingers brushing the ass he longed to grasp.

"I have a situation I need help with. Will you trust me to try something?"

Her eyes pulled him in. He could happily fall into them and gaze into their pale blue-green depths forever. She nodded. He slid his fingers into her hair, grasping the back of her head. His lips touched hers, tasting vanilla from the cake he'd watched her eat earlier. The taste and feel of finally having her in his arms had him hardening enough to pound nails. She squirmed against him, rubbing against his zipper.

He pulled away, gazing in her eyes. "You said we're friends and we obviously have chemistry."

"Yes, but..."

His finger stilled her words, rubbing along her top lip.

"I need your help as your friend. I never really planned on having to ask someone this but I'm still inexperienced. I heard you and your sisters talking so I know you have some experience. Will you teach me about sex?"

His alcohol-soaked brain catalogued her eyes filling with heat. He hoped that meant she was going to say yes. He wasn't sure how he'd survive if she said no.

The End

Bear stood beside Whiskey wondering how he ended up here. He loved his family and they'd had some ups and downs but today was ripping his heart out. How did he let her go? Is this what all parents felt?

"Have you set up any of the brothers to secretly follow them?" Whiskey whispered.

"No. Winnie heard me talking last week and told me she'd cut me off for a month if I ruined this."

Whiskey chuckled. "Yep, mine, too. I never dreamed I'd feel so protective. I've never been so happy when my middle one decided he loved the bar. One less thing to worry about."

Winnie's arm slipped through his, her head leaning on his shoulder. She still looked as beautiful today as the day he married her. Sure, they carried a little more weight and had more gray hairs but she was his sunbeam no matter how old they got.

"What are you two planning?" Winnie asked.

"For once, nothing, though it's only your threat that is keeping me from sending a couple prospects to watch them."

Winnie shook her head, rolling her eyes. "Our girl could clock any of the prospects within a couple miles of leaving. You all need to send them through our training if you want them to actually be good at what they do. Listen, she's gone on multiple security jobs and proven herself. She's tough and better than I ever was. They'll be fine together. Besides, we planned something to distract you guys."

Whiskey's woman cuddled up next to him. He dropped a kiss on her head. "Does it involve a bed?"

She laughed. "No, but it does involve something that vibrates between your legs."

Bear chuckled. "Where are we riding to?"

Winnie's face gave nothing away but he knew his woman long enough that he was going to love the answer. "We're taking a group ride to Kansas City. Leaving in two hours and if we happen to drop by our Topeka security office on the way, it will be a bonus."

Leave it to his woman to think up something that not only would take his mind off his oldest leading her first security detail but also put them within driving distance to be her backup if needed. Phoebe walked over to him. She'd changed so much from the five-year-old who had first thrown her arms around his neck telling him her mom was gone.

She'd grown into a strong, capable woman who along with some of her cousins were beginning to take over the bail bonds and security company.

"Dad, Mom, I love you and know you're worried." She wrapped her arms around Bear's middle and leaned on his chest. "You've given me every advantage and I'm prepared. That being said, I know you all are going on a long ride. I arranged for you all to have the back room at the Mexican restaurant you like so you can enjoy some good food while you wait. Just don't step in unless I request it."

He patted his daughter's back, realizing she was prepared. "It's just hard, Pheebs, when your little lightning bugs fly free. Someday you'll understand. Love you and go kick some ass."

"Swear jar." Phoebe giggled and held out her hand.

"Yo, Pheebs, get a move on. I want to have lunch in Wichita."

Phoebe kissed his cheek and hugged her mom. "Love you guys. Gotta go. Bad guys to catch and survivors to rescue."

Phoebe ran toward the SUV and hopped in the driver's side. She started it up and waved as she backed out and drove away. Being a parent was hard but he knew his girl had it.

"Dad, come on. You promised us range time and Mom said you're leaving in a couple hours." His two sons and his youngest daughter waited patiently by their motorcycles. He had it all and he owed it to his persistent sunbeam.

The End until Scoop's book

Thank you for reading Bear. If you loved he and Winnie's story, if you could rate or review it, your honest review will help future readers decide if they want to take a chance on a new-to-them author. I can't thank you enough for taking a chance on this new series. There are a lot more stories coming in the Bluff Creek Brotherhood Mc.

Scoop is the next in series. I've included a little excerpt here.

Scoop kept an eye on the woman he'd been falling for. Straight up head over heels, he couldn't imagine ever being happy without her. Add in the fact that no matter what woman was around or how skimpily she was dressed, he didn't get hard. Nope, his dick only perked up when she was around. And man, when she leaned over him to point out something on the computer, her hair falling across his shoulder smelling of vanilla, the fucker turned hard as steel. And if she had her blonde hair up in a messy bun on top of her head and her computer glasses on, his dick thought it was time to play ravish the hot librarian.

Too bad there were two things wrong with that scenario. First, he was positive he was in her friend zone. Being friends with the woman he couldn't get off his mind was a great start, but it wasn't where he wanted to stay. And second, he had zero experience ravishing a woman. A thirty-five-year-old virgin that hadn't even had a blow job. He didn't have any special reason. When he would have been going out in high school and later college, he was helping to raise his younger twin sisters and working two part time jobs for food on their table. His mom had struggled after his dad had left them. She'd worked a job while attending school to become a nurse. Scoop had done what he could to help them survive. There wasn't any time for extras like dating. Then he was focused on getting into the police academy. Once he finally had some time to himself, he hadn't connected with anyone. If he'd waited that long to finally take care of his pesky virginity, he didn't want to just bang one out in a bar bathroom though if she gave him the time of day- he'd do it anywhere.

To be that close to her, expose each delicious inch of her creamy skin and taste her would be his dream. Too bad he had no idea what to do. He'd never even asked a woman out.

Cannon was across the room talking to her. Scoop had never wanted to hit one of his friends more than when she laughed at something he said, tucking her hair behind her ear. Scoop was positive Cannon wasn't interested in her, but he envied the easy way Cannon flirted.

She was the whole package- brains, a hour glass figure he wanted to explore and a personality that had him craving her presence.

Flick tapped him on the shoulder. "When are you going to make your move?"

Scoop shook his head, tossed back another drink. He wasn't sure what number drink it was, but everything was getting nice and fuzzy. Fuzzy helped because then it didn't hurt so much if she ignored him. "She thinks I'm a friend. She doesn't see me like that."

Flick sipped his beer then tilted the bottle toward her. "Then build on that. Friends, then friends with benefits. You could ask her to help you with a favor. Getting rid of a certain status you have. Then when she falls for all the deliciousness of Mint Chocolate Chip, slip a ring on her finger and walk her down the aisle before she comes out of the sex daze."

Flick was a prankster and Scoop wasn't sure if he was serious or not. He might like her calling him that name but no one else was allowed. He was fine with the name Scoop.

They wouldn't be changing it to any of the ice cream flavors she called him.

"Are you joking or really suggesting I should do that?" Sober he had a hard time knowing if Flick was joking. He was well past happy drunk and moving into not feeling any pain drunk. Flick was going to have to be a little clearer for Scoop to understand.

Flick laid his hand on Scoop's shoulder. "Man, you've been falling for her since the first time you all collaborated on tech stuff. Think about this- do you want to be her friend and then maybe watch someone else romance her or do you want to go after the woman who puts a look on your face I've never seen before?"

He nodded, then swallowed. His mouth was dry despite the amount of liquor he'd consumed, and his heart pounded loud enough his chest felt like he was near the speakers at a rock concert. He licked his lip then decided to hell with it. The worst that could happen is she'd say no. He grabbed another drink and downed it. A little liquid courage was needed for this. He weaved over to where Sarah was standing in her dress from the wedding. It highlighted her breasts with her cleavage on display. He imagined diving in and pleasing her anyway he could. Cannon had walked away.

"Could I talk to you about something?" He worked to keep his words from slurring. The lights they'd hung to give Remington her dream lit Sarah's hair like a halo. She was so beautiful.

Sarah didn't answer right away, gazing into his eyes. She must have found the answer she needed because she nodded. She headed to the side of the yard, closer to the orchard entrance. He followed behind her trying to enjoy the sight of her rounded bubble butt cupped by her bridesmaids dress, but he was focusing on not throwing up. What if he ruined everything? What if she laughed at him? He wasn't sure he could handle her ridicule.

She paused at the entrance to the orchard. "What do you need?"

What did he need? He needed to cup her face in his hands, lay his lips against her and claim her. He wanted to see if she tasted as good as she smelled.

"I need to know if you'd be willing to help me with something."

Sarah smiled at him. Why did his heart feel better when she smiled? They could be frustrated and searching for a thread of information. She'd smile and bam, everything was better.

"Sure, if I can. Whatcha need Rocky Road?"

"It's a huge favor and I honestly don't know what to say." His skin felt too tight and he was sweating. Hopefully she couldn't see it on his forehead.

"How about you just ask?"

Ask. He could do that, but he couldn't wait another minute. He stepped closer, sliding his arm around her waist. Man, she smelled good. The sweet smell of cookies and banana bread. The smell that made you hungry to gorge yourself on sweets. It's what he wanted to do with Sarah. Gorge himself until he was satisfied. Her full breasts pressed against his chest.

"I see you as a friend I can trust, and I have a situation I need help with. Will you trust me to try something?"

Her eyes pulled him in. He could happily fall into them and gaze into their pale blue-green depths forever. She nodded.

He slid his fingers into her hair, grasping the back of her head. His lips touched hers, tasting vanilla from the cake he'd watched her eat earlier. The taste and feel of finally having her in his arms had him hardening enough to pound nails. She squirmed against him, rubbing against his zipper. If only he had the right to take her back to his room and unwrap her from her dress. Her lips were everything he'd imagined and he wanted to continue kissing her but he had a question.

He pulled away, gazing in her eyes, breathing a little heavier. "You said we're friends and we obviously have chemistry."

"Yes, but..."

His finger stilled her words, rubbing along her top lip. Her soft lips against his finger had him wondering if she was this soft all over. Her face blurred a little. Maybe he'd had little more than he should but he'd craved this for so long. He wasn't stopping now.

"I never really planned on having to ask someone this but I'm still inexperienced. I heard you and your sisters talking so I know you're not. Will you teach me about sex?"

His alcohol-soaked brain catalogued her eyes filling with heat. He hoped that meant she was going to say yes. He wasn't sure how he'd survive if she said no.

His trailed his fingers down her cheek, the smooth skin of her neck calling his name. Her neck wavered and then there were two of her necks. Hmmm, double his pleasure.

"Scoop, are you okay?" Sarah's voice came from far away. His vision darkened and he reached for Sarah. He needed something from her. What had they been talking about?

Oh man, his stomach was roiling. He pulled away from Sarah. What had they been talking about? He realized he wasn't going to stop his stomach. He moved away from Sarah, turning to the side and bending at the waist as all the alcohol and food made a reappearance. The smell it made as it splashed onto the ground and up onto his pants and shoes had him vomiting some more.

Then everything started to darken. Oh fuck.

Scoop isn't up for preorder yet. The best way to stay in touch is to be a part of my newsletter. If you aren't on my list yet, grab my free prequel here: https://dl.bookfunnel.com/fbvhukvk7f

You'll get a free book. I share excerpts as I'm writing and you'll be the first to know when Scoop is up for preorder.

Once again, thank you so much for reading Bear.

Regina's Gravy Steak Recipe

Regina's gravy steak recipe comes from my mom. We always had it with mashed potatoes and hot rolls. I loved walking into the kitchen and smelling it cooking. Due to some food allergies I developed later in life, I've modified it so I can still have it. I'm giving you both recipes. Hers is a lot easier. I cook mine like my mom does in an electric skillet. My brother does his in a pan in the oven. The electric skillet requires you to stir and scrape the bottom of the pan about every 15 minutes. If you end up trying one of them, let me know what you think.

<u>Mom's gravy steak</u>

Ingredients

4-6 pieces of minute steak(called cube steak or tenderized round steak)

2 cans of Campbell's cream of mushroom soup/ Or Nat's homemade cream of mushroom listed below*

3+ cans of hot water

Dash of Lawry's seasoning salt

2 shakes of black pepper

*Nat's homemade cream of mushroom soup-

1 Tbsp. butter or butter type spread

2 cubes of bouillon (I use the Not Chick'N by Edward & sons)

1 can pieces and stems mushrooms chopped

4 cups almond milk

2-4 Tbsp. corn starch

Mix all ingredients with whisk. Heat in microwave or on top of stove. Stir every thirty seconds in microwave. Stir constantly on stove.

For the minutes steaks-

Spray electric skillet with non-stick spray, turn heat to 350 degrees.

Place steaks on hot skillet, lightly season with seasoning salt and pepper. Brown on one side. Flip, brown on second side. Depending on your skillet, it will probably take about 2-3 minutes each side.

Then add 2 cans of hot water and then use rubber spatula to loosen any browning's from the pan. The water will turn beige or light brown which is perfect.

Stir in the two cans of Campbell's soup or add Nat's homemade cream of mushroom soup.

See where liquid is on side of pan and how thick. Liquid needs to completely cover the steak and be liquid enough it simmers but doesn't boil and pop out of the skillet.

Turn skillet down to 275-300. Check every fifteen minutes. Stir the skillet and scrap the bottom to make sure it's not sticking. If you're making with cream of mushroom soup, it tend to stick less than if you're using my homemade recipe. Steaks will be done in about an hour and thirty minutes. But... if you want them like they are described in the book, then patience is key. Let them cook for at least two hours.

If you don't want to keep stirring the electric skillet, you can transfer them to a pan and cook them at 325 degrees in the oven. The longer they cook, the more tender they will be.

Because my family loves the gravy on bread and mashed potatoes, I sometimes split the steak into two skillets if we have a lot of people coming over because then I double the gravy recipe. I never want to ration their gravy for their mashed potatoes.

I hope you enjoy it as much as my family does.